Sign up for our newsletter to hear about new and upcoming releases.

www.ylva-publishing.com

Pinned by Love

Elaine J Daniels

Dedication

To wrestling fans, new and old.
To those who want double the sapphic monster action.
And to my wife, who planted this seed in my noggin.

Content Warnings

Pinned by Love is a low-angst romance with an HEA. However, please note that this book contains sexually explicit content, including exhibitionism. If you wish to skip, or just want to be prepared, the chapters containing smut are: 12, 15, 16, 19, and 26.

Author's Note

This story takes place in a fantasy monster realm. Humans exist in this realm but only because they have slipped through the cracks that separate humans and monsters. As a result, different aspects of each era of professional wrestling overlap and intermingle.

Pro wrestling is widely known to be scripted now, but the most important thing you should know is that for years, there was a culture of never breaking character (also known as kayfabe), and even to this day, some pro wrestlers choose not to break kayfabe or pull back the curtain too far.

I want this story to be accessible to everyone, even readers with little to no wrestling entertainment knowledge. Here are a few terms in wrestling entertainment that you need to know:

- **Babyface/face:** the hero
- **Heel:** the villain
- **Stage name:** the name a wrestling entertainer uses when performing. This is different from the legal name they use in their personal lives
- **Promo:** a dialogue-heavy segment that's meant to advance the storyline
- **Heat:** a negative reaction from the crowd toward the wrestlers

Character Appendix

Hopefully, throughout the story, I have made clear the different names, stage names, and nicknames for the wrestlers. But just in case I haven't, here is this little character appendix for reference.

Iris

- Harpy
- Heel
- Stage name: Athena "The Snatcher" Rainstorm

Lena

- Minotaur
- Babyface
- Stage name: Helen "Mother" Stronghorn

Daphne

- Satyr
- Heel
- Stage name: Fauna "The Dancer" Piper

Gianna

- Wolven
- Babyface
- Stage name: Luna "The Alpha" Thrasher

June

- Dragon
- Babyface
- Stage name: Eileen "The Empress" Waterclaw

Pan

- Demon
- Heel
- Stage name: Lil "The Temptation" Nightheart

Chapter 1

Iris

"ATHENA! ATHENA! DO YOU HAVE time for a few words?"

An overeager voice shouts from behind me as I make my way down the barren hallways toward the arena's staging area.

I inhale a deep, calming breath before turning around, offering what I hope is a winning smile to the camera being shoved in my face. The goal is to look cool and confident, but on the inside my stomach twists and my heart pounds. Today's match has been predetermined, like all matches in Elite Monster Wrestling, and yet I still have to pretend I don't know who will win. But that's not what upsets me.

It's the fact that I'm about to step out into that arena and listen to the crowd boo and hiss as the announcer calls my name. Unfortunately, that's the burden a heel must bear.

Hazel, the blonde wood nymph in charge of backstage interviews, holds a microphone to my mouth, her overpowering perfume tickling my nose. "Athena Rainstorm, the last time you faced Eileen Waterclaw, you almost tasted defeat. What did you do to prepare for a win in tonight's main event?"

Squaring my shoulders, I glare down the lens of the camera. "The biggest difference between the Athena Rainstorm who faces Eileen Waterclaw today and the Athena Rainstorm who faced her last time is that I'm no longer holding back." I snap my wings to drive home my point. "Waterclaw better watch out because she is in for a world of pain."

I've been a heel since I started my career, and playing one comes naturally to me. But what started as a fun and cheeky way to claw my way up the ranks of the EMW has lately turned sour.

Hazel's forest-green eyes sparkle. "But The Empress has been taken under the wing of Helen Stronghorn since your last match. Aren't you at all afraid of a dragon who has been trained by such an unstoppable force in the EMW?"

My eye roll is genuine, but I play it up for the camera. Fuck Helen Stronghorn and the pegasus she flew in on! But I can't say that. F-bombs on live television are a big no-no.

Instead, I respond, "And you think I'm scared of Helen?" I tap my temple. "That minotaur has nothing going on between the horns but open range. I would take on her and her little protégé, Eileen, at the same time and still come out on top."

"Bold words from someone who hasn't faced Mother in years." Hazel smirks, knowing she's hit a sore spot both in and out of storyline.

Most of us on the roster get along off-screen. Heels and faces may not be allowed to comingle anywhere publicly—to maintain the illusion that the rivalries and drama are real—but we can all be friendly behind closed doors.

But it's no secret among EMW's wrestlers and staff that Lena—also known as Helen "Mother" Stronghorn—and I don't get along. In fact, you could probably say we downright hate each other. At least on my end; I don't bother talking to Lena long enough to find out how she really feels about me.

I flash my fangs. Hazel is pissing me off, but that's part of her job. She's supposed to "fire us up" before matches to sell our rivalries to the audience, but it sucks that it's actually working.

The good news is that, as the heel, I'm allowed to be a bitch to anyone and everyone, even the innocent (and not-so-innocent) interviewers.

With a menacing glare, I jab my index finger toward Hazel's chest. "Mark my words, wood nymph, destroying Eileen Waterclaw puts me one step closer to taking down Helen Stronghorn and all she stands for."

Hazel's eyes dance in the shitty fluorescent lighting; this promo will be well received. But she has to sell it, so she sucks in a breath and leans away from me, playing the role of uncomfortable interviewer. I use this opportunity to end the conversation.

"Now, if you'll excuse me"—I curl my lips, baring my teeth—"I have a match to win." Flipping my hair over my shoulder, I glare at the camera once more before sauntering down the hall with my head held high.

As soon as I turn the corner, safely out of the camera's view, I lean my back against the cool concrete wall and let out a long sigh. Thank the goddess that's over. Every time I do one of those promos, where I'm forced to pretend to be cruel, it chips away at my soul. It's exhausting pretending to be that vicious.

"Hey there, Iris." I'm greeted by the soft voice of Pan.

I glance toward the approaching demon, known widely by their stage name of Lil Nightheart. Their red skin glistens with sweat, and their chest heaves. They just lost a match against the werewolf Luna Thrasher, a very grumpy yet kind Wolven.

"Did Gianna kick your ass?" I ask with a grin, referring to Luna by her legal name.

Pan grits their teeth, rubbing their left shoulder. "She may have pulled a little too hard during her armbar, but no real harm. She already apologized."

My brow furrows. "Do you need a medic?"

"Nah!" They wave me off. "But I didn't come over here to talk about me."

"Ugh!" I exclaim with a groan, fisting my hair. "I'm just trying to relax before I have to go out there."

My friend holds up their hands and takes a step back. "I hear you; I hear you. I just wanted to make sure you're okay."

I narrow my eyes. "Why wouldn't I be?"

"Because it's obvious how burned-out you are." They cock their head to the side, their short, inky black bob brushing against their chin.

My wings sag. "You're right. I don't know how much longer I can do—"

"Iris!" A sharp and urgent voice interrupts me. A troll with a clipboard and headphones rushes down the hall toward me.

"Oh shit," I murmur, looking around for a clock. I must be late if the EMW producers sent an assistant to find me.

"'Oh shit' is right!" the troll huffs, out of breath from his sprint. "We gotta go! You're on in three minutes."

Pan shoots me an empathic half smile. I straighten my back and lift my chin before following the flustered production assistant.

Like it or not, it's time.

Let's do this.

Chapter 2

Virginia Lavender

Nikolas Thistle and I sit at the commentator table, peering at the screens that give us the current camera view for the audience back home. Sometimes I wish I could just watch the match organically, but the biggest part of my job is to commentate on what's happening for our television audience, which means speaking into this tiny mic and paying attention to these tiny screens.

The bell rings three times.

"Introducing first, from the mountain of the Harpy Clan, Athena 'The Snatcher' Rainstorm!" The voice of the orc ring announcer, Ivy, echoes throughout the stadium while jeers from the crowd rumble the floor.

The harpy smirks at the spectators, unbothered by their obvious disdain. With a flip of her dark-gray hair over her shoulder, she saunters to the ring, her black, low-cut spandex leotard gleaming in the arena's bright lights. I have to admit, she looks hot. Athena is a total smoke show.

"A woman on a mission, Athena is ready to prove she can earn the Elite Monster Wrestling Championship. What do you think, Virginia?" Nikolas says with the enthusiasm only a professional wrestling commentator can muster.

I lean toward Nikolas, a burly griffin, who dwarfs my small moth-person frame. "It won't be easy for The Snatcher," I point out, my delicate wings fluttering behind me. "You have to put in the effort and prove you're ready and capable of a championship match. She has quite the roster to run through first, starting with tonight's fight."

Nikolas cocks his head. "Do you think Athena has what it takes?"

"We'll certainly know more after tonight's match."

Athena finishes her stroll to the ring, looks into the camera and licks her lips before ducking under the ropes to enter. She stands, opening her wings, patterned like that of a gray hawk's, with a sharp snap, showcasing her impressive wingspan to the audience. They boo, drowning out her intro music, a heavy metal song with melodic vocals.

"Hate her or love her, you can't deny Athena's near-perfect physical form. She's a true athlete," I remark.

Nikolas tuts. "Do you hear the crowd? There's no love there."

The music changes to a bubblegum pop song with cutesy vocals, and Athena rolls her eyes, crossing her arms over her ample chest.

"And her opponent," Ivy's voice blares through the arena speakers. "From the oceans of the Dragon Clan, Eileen 'The Empress' Waterclaw!"

The tall and lithe dragon dances out from behind the LED walls, flashing her sharp teeth with a large smile. She glides to the stage, slapping the hands of her adoring fans as they reach for her over the barricade.

"Listen to the crowd!" Nikolas exclaims. "They want to see The Empress take down Rainstorm."

I nod, my antennae twitching. "It will be tough. Eileen is a flier as well, but she doesn't have the power behind her dives that Athena does."

"It's the lack of wings." The griffin tsks. "If only dragons had wings instead of floating on air."

"That doesn't stop her from being a formidable foe," I snap, playing the role of babyface enthusiast, even though personally, I'm more of a fan of Athena's wrestling style. "Athena can't underestimate her."

Eileen floats over the ropes and lands in front of Athena. Her jade-green scales and golden locks shine, contrasting against the glittering deep-blue spandex of her hot pants and crop top combo. She stares down the harpy, a confident gleam in her onyx eyes.

"The last time Eileen and Athena were in the ring together, The Snatcher came out on top," I explain. "But Eileen hopes in tonight's match to showcase her hard work and dedication to becoming a better wrestler by destroying Athena."

A short yet muscular human official with a shaved head joins them, checking that both wrestlers are ready.

"Let's do this!" Eileen pumps a clawed fist in the air.

Athena just nods, never taking her violet eyes off the dragon.

The bell dings three times.

Eileen snaps her long, tufted tail against the ring's floor, causing Athena to bounce a few inches in the air before she comes slamming back down in a fighting stance.

"Are you sure you can take me on?" Eileen taunts. "You may have won last time, but Helen has been training me since then. You think you're hot shit, but your reign of terror ends here tonight."

"You talk too much," Athena growls before charging Eileen.

The two monsters collide, gripping each other by the back of the necks.

I clap my hands. "And here we go."

Eileen slips to the right, ducking out of Athena's grasp before driving her knee into the harpy's gut.

Nikolas winces. "Ouch! A knee by The Empress into the gut of The Snatcher."

Collapsing to the ground, Athena clutches her stomach and groans. The crowd cheers, clearly thrilled Waterclaw got the first hit.

Eileen grabs Athena's hair by the scalp, lifting her so that the dragon can send a fist flying straight into the harpy's face. Athena stumbles back at the punch, clutching her nose.

"That took some of the wind out of Rainstorm," I remark. "She looks unsure on her feet."

"Oh!" Nikolas jumps to the edge of his seat as Athena takes a backhanded fist from Eileen and flies into the ropes. "Can Eileen capitalize on this turn of events?"

Eileen runs to the opposite side of the ring, presses her back against the ropes, and uses the momentum to sprint toward Athena, but the harpy ducks, narrowly missing the elbow aimed for her face. Eileen looks around with knitted brows, and Athena uses the opportunity to snatch Eileen's horns.

Nikolas snaps his beak in excitement. "Athena is setting up."

Athena scoops Eileen by the armpits before rolling the dragon over her chest until Eileen straddles her shoulders.

"Here it goes!" I leap from my chair, anxious to see one of Athena's powerful displays of strength.

Athena slams Eileen to the ring's floor.

"Powerbomb!" Nikolas and I exclaim at the same time.

Eileen doesn't move, her head lolling to the side. Athena drops to the ground and presses all her weight onto her opponent before hooking her elbow behind one of Eileen's knees and leaning back. She's pinned the dragon's shoulders to the floor.

At that, the official kneels, slamming their hand as they begin the count. The audience happily joins in.

"One! Two! Thr—!"

The crowd cheers as Eileen kicks out.

I scoff. "Rainstorm should know better than to think she can take down Waterclaw that easily."

Athena lets out a scream through clenched teeth as she slams her fists against the ring floor, clearly lamenting the win that slipped through her fingertips. Meanwhile, Eileen struggles to stand. She reaches for the ropes to assist her recovery.

"The Snatcher better watch out," Nikolas says just before Eileen drops an elbow on the back of Athena's neck.

The harpy lands face first, a pained groan escaping her throat. But Eileen doesn't allow her any reprieve; instead, she assaults the back of Athena's head with an onslaught of quick stomps.

I flap my wings. This match just got interesting. "Athena's in trouble now. When Eileen gets going like this, she's nearly unstoppable."

Then, as if a fire is lit under her, Athena rolls out of the way, sending Eileen's claws crashing to the ring floor without even the cushion of a body underneath her. Boos from the crowd drown out the dragon's howls, as she clutches her paw, hopping one leg away from Athena.

"What a devastating blow." Nikolas winces. "Eileen may be enthusiastic about taking on Athena, but she has to remember her opponent's experience—and that maneuver Athena just pulled shows it."

While Eileen tests her weight on her injured paw, Athena ascends the ropes, her back to her opponent. Once at the top, she extends her feathered wings and arms wide. The crowd roars.

I feel my brow furrow. "What is Athena doing now?"

With a wink to the displeased crowd, Athena bends her knees, shoving off the top rope into a backflip. Looking magnificent and graceful, she flaps her wings, giving her the air to arch over Eileen's head before slamming her talons into the dragon's face.

"Athena connects!" Nikolas snaps his wings. "Will this be it for Waterclaw?"

Eileen stumbles back, hands covering her nose. The harpy lands gracefully on her taloned feet, baring her teeth at her opponent. The crowd boos as Athena grabs Eileen by the mane, dragging her to the edge of the ring. With a hard kick to Eileen's hip, Athena sends the dragon tumbling over the top rope.

"Eileen's been sent to the outside by Athena, and she's landed right in front of our announcer table." I fidget, ready to jump out of the way to avoid collision with the wrestlers. They would never hurt us on purpose, but they often get so involved in the match that they don't pay attention. It's up to me and Nikolas to be vigilant.

"And here comes Athena!" Nikolas whoops as the harpy dives out of the ring and straddles the writhing dragon.

Athena slams her fists into her opponent's temples. Eileen throws up her hands, attempting to block the onslaught. With a roar, the dragon bucks her hips, knocking Athena off balance. Athena flaps her wings, scrambling to flee Eileen's reach, but Eileen snatches Athena by the throat.

"Waterclaw won't let Rainstorm escape!" I shout. This aggression from Waterclaw is new and exciting.

Keeping her grip on Athena's neck, Eileen uses her power of dragon levitation to hover off the ground, hauling her opponent back toward the ring. She tosses Athena under the bottom rope. The harpy pins her wings and rolls into the ring, now desperate to escape the dragon.

Another of Eileen's impressive dragon roars rumbles the arena, and the crowd goes wild, fans cheering her on as she leaps between the ropes, reaching for Athena.

"Eileen has Athena right where she wants her." Nikolas flicks his lion tail, nodding toward Eileen, who's now lifted Athena above her head.

The dragon lets out a shriek of laughter before slamming the harpy onto the mat face-first. Athena's wings droop to the floor.

Nikolas grips my shoulder in anticipation. "I think this is it for The Snatcher."

Eileen drops to the mat, folding Athena's legs toward her chest to pin her opponent's shoulders to the floor. The official kneels and begins their count.

The crowd counts along with each slam of their hand.

"One! Tw—!"

But Athena kicks out, sending Eileen onto her back.

"Eileen is unable to bring it home," I grumble as the crowd boos, despite being secretly excited the match is continuing.

While Athena drags herself to the ropes to recover, Eileen stares at her, mouth agape and breathing hard.

The fans begins their signature chant for Eileen, spurring on their heroine. "Lucky! Lucky! Lucky!"

Eileen stands, holding her paws in the air, offering the crowd a winning smile. She's so busy preening for the audience that she doesn't see Athena recover and come running at her, elbow cocked back. Eileen notices her opponent too late, and Athena's fist slams into Eileen's nose. The dragon falls back, crashing onto her back with a groan.

"That has got to hurt." Nikolas looks away. "But once again, Eileen forgot she was up against a veteran like Athena."

Athena claws herself up the ropes with slow and deliberate movements, her chest heaving. When she reaches the top, she closes her eyes momentarily, as if gathering herself.

I point to Eileen, who is still rolling around on the floor. "Eileen Waterclaw needs to move, or she will face the wrath of Rainstorm."

"Will she escape Athena's warpath?" Nikolas fidgets, eyes trained on Athena as she crouches on the top rope.

Athena inhales before springing upward with a scream, beginning her descent toward Eileen with her wings tucked behind her, her forearm out in front .

Nikolas clenches his claws. “Here comes the flying elbow!”

A slam reverberates through the arena as Athena crashes to the floor, elbow connecting with Eileen’s chest. Eileen’s head lolls to the side as Athena grunts and repositions herself to kneel before her opponent. She then drapes Eileen’s legs over her shoulders, pinning the dragon’s back to the mat.

Eileen doesn’t react, still disoriented from Athena’s brutal elbow, and the fans roar, leaping to their feet as the official begins their countdown yet again.

“Will Eileen Waterclaw kick out of this one?” I ask, also rising from my chair, adding a thread of worry to my voice for the viewers at home.

“One!” the audience counts when the official connects their hand with the mat.

Another slap. “Two!”

But Eileen doesn’t move. Athena smirks as the official’s hands smack onto the mat for the third and final time. I put my hand over my face to hide a smirk of my own.

“Three!”

“Athena Rainstorm for the win!” Nikolas roars.

The bell dings three times, announcing the match’s end. She drops Eileen’s legs before flapping her wings and soaring into the air over the ring, fist pumped above her head. The crowd screams in awe and disappointment at their heroine’s downfall. They had hoped to see Athena’s reign of terror come to an end.

“Just listen to the people!” I shout over the crowd’s roar. “They’re going to bring down the arena!”

Nikolas snorts. “They’ll just have to get over it. Athena’s athletic ability is unmatched.”

“You’re forgetting about Helen Stronghorn,” I narrow my eyes at him. “Do you really think Athena can take down the EMW Realms Champion?”

I look back at the action. Snapping her wings, Athena dives for the exit, flashing her fangs with a toothy grin. The crowd boos, throwing various lewd gestures toward the victorious harpy as she flies out of the arena.

Nikolas ruffles his feathers. "After Athena's performance tonight, I think she will give Mother a run for her money."

Chapter 3

Iris

The muscles that control my wings strain as I descend, doing my best to make my landing graceful. You never know where an interviewer might be lurking. My eyes dart around the staging area as I search for any signs of cameras. The coast is clear. It's just the crowd of production assistants and medics clamoring to make sure I'm okay.

I finally let go of the breath I've been holding and allow myself to suck in the cooler air. The arena lights are always hot, and I'm drenched in sweat, not only from their scorching heat but from the exertion of the match. No matter how much I train and practice, putting on a good show for the audience is no walk in the park. Every stunt takes a toll on my body, even with textbook-perfect execution. On top of that, we have to *act* because while hits and bumps still hurt, we have to play it up for the crowd.

It's a lot to handle at once, and I'm always impressed with my fellow wrestlers. It takes years of training to excel at it all.

My chest's deep and rapid heaves finally start to dissipate when June, or Eileen Waterclaw as the world knows her, appears, dragging herself into the staging area. When she sees there are no cameras, she lets out a sigh of relief and straightens her posture.

"Hey, Iris," she chirps, offering me a tentative smile. "Great match!"

I return her grin, genuinely happy she's unharmed. Sometimes freak accidents happen. Sometimes we get sloppy.

"Thanks! I'm glad we practiced that powerbomb."

She barks a laugh, shoulders relaxing. "Oh, my goddess! Yes! That could have really hurt otherwise."

The same troll production assistant that fetched me earlier approaches and clears his throat. "Iris, Mr. Palmer wants to speak to you."

My heart skips a beat. "Now?"

"Not right this instant," the troll huffs. "No need to bring your sweaty feathers into his office. He expects you within the hour."

And with a curt turn on his heel, the troll dashes toward the other production assistants, ready to break down the arena now that the main event is over.

June grimaces, exposing her sharp fangs. "Yikes. I wonder what that's about."

Charles Palmer is like some sort of genius cockroach. He slipped into our realm, the 'monster realm' as he calls it, from the human one roughly thirty years ago with two things: a dream and a tenacious determination to succeed. With surprising speed, he charmed investors and secured the funds and the power to build the EMW into what it is today. While he's a total slimeball who only cares about money, no one can deny his ability to manage a successful entertainment business.

And I'm not looking forward to meeting with him at all. It means my career is about to change—for better or for worse.

It's a bit of a bummer I have to rush to get ready as the locker room in this arena is spotless and smells of lemon cleaning products. It would have been nice to participate in some self-care after such a grueling match.

I speed through my shower and preen my feathers instead of taking my time as usual. I want to get this conversation over with as soon as possible. As I twist my damp hair into a long braid, I concentrate on my positive traits as a professional wrestler.

For one, I'm a safe opponent. I haven't accidentally hurt anyone since my developmental days. For another, I put on a good show. The crowd loves to hate me, and they pack the arena whenever I'm headlining, eager to see my demise. Too bad for them, I'm on a winning streak.

By all means, I should be hopeful. Charles has no reason to demote me. But I didn't get to where I'm at now in professional wrestling by being all sunshine and rainbows.

I got here by working harder than everyone else because I had to. Not only is training and schooling expensive but you also have to dedicate a lot of time. And I didn't come from money or an established wrestling family.

Unlike Lena, better known as Helen Stronghorn.

The Minotaur is the doll of the EMW, all because of her legendary daddy, The Mighty Minos. He was a hero of mine growing up, so when I met his daughter, I expected to respect her as much as I respect him.

Nope. Lena sucks.

She didn't spend her time on the independent circuit paying her dues. Instead, Lena waltzed right in, gaining a babyface persona, immediate upward trajectory, and instant stardom.

It also doesn't help that she's a total brat.

I'm talking entitled, bossy, and downright snooty. The first time I witnessed Lena throw a fit, I couldn't believe what I was seeing. She straight-up lost it on the hair and makeup artist for not giving her russet curls enough bounce.

"I need to sell the hits!" she snarled, bringing the werecat artist to tears. "Do you think I can do that with this flat hair?"

Thankfully, the lead production assistant smoothed things over before I could stomp my way over there and give Lena a piece of my mind.

I shake my head. Time to stop stewing about her. I slip a silky, blue blouse over my shoulders, custom-made to accommodate the wings above my hips.

With a deep breath, I step out of the locker room. I hold my head high as I navigate the bustling halls to Charles's office, avoiding eye contact so I don't get sucked into any small talk with my fellow wrestlers. Everyone lets me pass. Probably the word has spread that the owner wants to see me. How irritating.

As if on cue, validating my suspicions, Daphne prances toward me, her hooves clacking on the concrete floor.

"Hey, Iris!" The satyr smiles, her brown skin and fur sparkling from all the glitter she applied before her smack-talking live promo against Lena earlier in the evening. "Good luck at your meeting with Old Man Palmer."

While I want to avoid most of my peers, Daphne is one of my best friends. She never fails to make me feel better with her infectious positivity.

The smile I return is genuine. "Thank you." I nudge her with my elbow. "How did your promo go?"

She's a newer addition to the roster, her storyline focusing on her overinflated ego and carefree attitude. Surprisingly, both characteristics apply to Daphne's real-life personality, but in a charming way I adore.

"It ended with me flat on my back thanks to a chokeslam from Lena, but it was worth it to be in the face of that fine piece of art sculpted by the goddess herself." Daphne winks.

I wrinkle my nose. "Ew. Can you not talk about Lena that way?"

"You just hate her too much to see how perfect she is." She cackles "Those beefy arms, that peach of an ass, and not to mention those big horns. How often do you see a female minotaur with horns like *that*?"

"I am once again asking you not to talk about Lena that way—especially about her ass."

Daphne waggles her eyebrows. "Just give her a good once-over the next time you see her and tell me I'm wrong."

I groan. "I'm no longer happy to see you. Please go away now."

"Oh, hush. You love me."

"You know I do," I respond with a soft smile.

Daphne stops in her tracks and lowers her voice. "Oh shit. We're almost at Charles's office. Drinks with me and Pan after?"

I nod. "Sounds great! I'll probably need it."

"Alrighty, then!" She blows me a kiss. "Talk to you later. And good luck!"

With a nod, I continue the last few feet to Charles's office door and nod to the human assistant standing outside. His name is Zach, and I've always thought he looks a bit like a weasel with his greasy dark hair, smudged glasses, sickly white skin, and beady black eyes.

He knocks on the door for me, alerting the boss to my presence. I brace myself, mentally preparing for whatever is about to happen.

"Come on in," answers Charles Palmer in his heavy southern accent.

I slowly open the door and step into his impossibly immaculate office space. It doesn't match the gray, dreary halls of the arena's backstage. No matter where we travel for shows, Charles always ends up in the cleanest room—one that looks like it was recently renovated and is always in his preferred colors of blood red and black. "Power colors," he boasts whenever anyone mentions the aesthetic.

Palmer leans forward on his desk at the sight of me, his large and imposing frame swallowing the flat surface. "Ah! Iris, my dear Athena Rainstorm!"

Charles likes confidence. Squaring my shoulders, I take the seat directly across from him. The man calls himself a proud Texan, and from what I've seen of human media, he looks like some sort of stereotype.

A bushy, gray, and perfectly manicured mustache sits above his thin lips, currently pulled back into a smile of dazzling white teeth that stand out against his healthy tan. He brushes a speck of invisible dirt from his tailored powder-blue suit with a matching ten-gallon hat that somehow complements his steely gray eyes. Top that all off with a head of thick, salt-and-pepper hair and you have yourself a handsome human.

Too bad he's a total skeeze ball and I don't trust him.

"You wanted to see me, sir?" I force a grin, willing myself not to flinch when his smile somehow becomes even wider, like a shark circling their floundering prey.

"Cutting right to the chase. I've always liked that about you." Charles chuckles before nodding to the CCTV mounted to the wall behind me. "I enjoyed your match against June."

"Thank you, sir."

He reaches beneath his desk and pulls out a bottle of whiskey and two glasses. "Drop the 'sir.' How long have you worked for me?"

"About ten years now."

"That makes you, what, in your mid thirties?" Charles asks, pouring three fingers of whiskey into each glass.

I nod. "I'm thirty-five."

"You're in your prime, especially for a monster. Harpies live about two hundred years, right? Can you believe that some humans start struggling with their physical health at your age." He hands me a glass.

"Thank you." I grip the glass in my hand. "What's this for?"

Charles laughs. "There you go with that directness. It's to toast to your success." He raises his glass. "I want you to headline MonsterMadness."

My composure falls apart as I begin to tremble. Me? Headline MonsterMadness? Could this really be happening?

This has been my dream since before I could fly. I can't believe I'm sitting across from Charles Palmer, a glass of celebratory whiskey in my hand, with an offer on the table to headline the biggest event in monster wrestling entertainment.

"Well?" Charles swirls the amber liquid in his glass. "Are you just going to gawk at me, or are you gonna say yes?"

Oh shit. In my disbelief, I forgot to say anything. "Of course! I would be honored to headline MonsterMadness, sir; I mean, Charles."

Charles reaches his glass toward me, signaling to me that it's time to toast. I meet him a little more than halfway with what I can only assume is a goofy-ass smile. My heart soars, and I fight back a giggle as I bring the glass to my lips.

The liquid burns my throat as it goes down. Despite that, this might be the best thing I've ever tasted. At this point, toilet water would be like fine wine. This moment is too sweet, too triumphant, for anything to spoil it.

"I anticipate this being the biggest MonsterMadness to date," he says. "When I came over from the human realm all those years ago, I dreamt that monster wrestling would one day be as big as the human version. Now, I haven't been back over, but the reports lead me to believe we're doing pretty good; but we could do better."

I lean forward in my seat, eager for any information about the human realm I can get. Humans and monsters can access different realms, but it's usually by accident or by very powerful magic. Information, culture details, and media gathered from the human realm are very rare and coveted. There are some who make a living traveling between the realms, but it takes a lot of effort.

I open my mouth to ask more about the human realm, the drink making me bold, when he cuts me off.

"Of course, you'll be going up against Helen Stronghorn," Charles announces before placing his empty glass on the desk with a soft clink. "And, of course, she's retaining the championship."

My stomach twists, the liquor suddenly sour in my stomach. No. This can't be. I've finally made it to MonsterMadness, and I have to lose.

To Lena.

I school my features, hoping Charles doesn't notice the roaring fire raging inside me. This is still an amazing opportunity for any wrestler in the industry. But not for me. Not like this.

The dazzling smile fades from Charles's face; his lips become a thin, flat line. "It's no secret how much you don't get along with Lena. It's my job to know what goes on with my staff and my athletes. I just didn't expect you to be so ungrateful, considering your background. Did we celebrate too early?"

I blanch. I'm totally fucked if I don't get this situation under control. "I'm not ungrateful, sir," I assure him. "I'm still in shock at even being offered this amazing opportunity."

"That's what I like to hear. You're quite the talent, and I would hate to see your career come to a halt because of a little grudge. I expect some maturity from my wrestlers."

I nod. "Of course, sir. No grudge here. Consider it water under the bridge."

He shoots me another one of his oily smiles. "Excellent, because you start training with her tomorrow."

"Tomorrow?" My question comes out as a squeak.

I was looking forward to a day or two off after tonight's match, not only to relax but also to cool down from the news.

Charles twirls his mustache between his thumb and forefinger. "When was the last time you faced Helen Stronghorn?"

"Our storylines haven't crossed in a few years." *Fuck.* I see where he's going with this.

"Exactly. I know you and Lena are both amazing improv wrestlers, but when was the last time you suplexed a minotaur?"

He's right. It's been a long time, and Lena is *tall* and much bigger than me. Unfortunately, I need the practice.

I hold my chin high, unwilling to let Charles know how upset I still am by the outcome of this meeting. "What time do we start tomorrow?"

His smile is warm—as if he didn't just threaten to end my career. "Now, I understand you need a little rest and time to fly back home, so I'll be generous. I expect to see you both in the practice ring by no later than noon tomorrow."

"Understood." I give him a curt nod. "I won't let you down."

"Of course you won't. Place your glass on the bottom shelf of that bar cart on your way out."

"Yes, sir."

He waves a dismissive hand. "It's 'Charles.' I'll see you tomorrow afternoon."

I don't bother responding. The conversation is over. My fate has been sealed.

With a soft click, the office door shuts behind me. I close my eyes, suddenly exhausted. Going from the highest high to the lowest low has really taken it out of me. Do I even want to have drinks with Daphne and Pan at this point? Honestly, I kind of want to head back to my hotel room, order room service, and watch whatever human anime they have on cable. I hope it's the one about the magical girls.

"Uhh…hey, Iris. I need to get in Charlie's office," says an all-too-familiar and annoying voice.

Can I catch a damn break?

I open my eyes to glare at the towering reddish-brown minotaur. Lena is still dressed in her match attire of sparkly sky-blue bikini bottoms, a triangle crop top, and chaps with silver accents. Why didn't she change into something more professional for a meeting with EMW's owner? Daphne and Lena didn't have an official match tonight, but they still exchanged a few blows and stunts. I know she's sweaty.

She frowns and waves her hand at the door in short, irritated movements.

I puff out my chest, standing as tall as I can. It does nothing against Lena's six-and-a-half-foot frame, but it does make me feel a little better. "You could ask politely, you know?"

"Like that would make you any less unpleasant." She rolls her eyes. "You would just find another stupid reason to attack me."

"Stupid?" My face and neck flush. How dare she call me stupid!

Lena smirks. "You heard me. Now, move. I need to talk to Charlie."

I roll my eyes. Of course she would be on a nickname basis with Charles Palmer. She's known him since she was a kid, thanks to her dad. Why would she follow the same rules and standards as the rest of us?

"Are you going to explain to him why I'm late?" she asks, crossing her arms over her chest.

My gaze rakes over her, sizing her up. It's been a while since I took a *really* good look at the great Helen Stronghorn. Proud curved horns sit atop a mound of bouncy curls the same color as her fur. Poking from between her russet strands are two long, sloping ears. Large brown eyes with impossibly long lashes are the star of her face, which ends in a round snout. Her figure is all curves and muscle with sculpted biceps, abs, and thighs contrasting her soft breasts and hips.

I remember Daphne's remark from earlier about the minotaur being a 'fine piece of art,' and my cheeks heat for a brand-new reason.

Fuck! My friend is right. Lena is gorgeous. And I hate it.

"Why are you looking at me like that?" Lena glares down at me.

I force a sneer. "Just making sure I can still take you on."

Lena takes a step back, her hooves clacking against the cement floor. "What do you mean by that?"

I flip my braid over my shoulder, not looking back as I saunter away, my tail feathers quivering. She'll know exactly what I mean in a few moments. For now, I'll take the victory of catching her off guard.

Chapter 4

Lena

My meeting with Charlie went better than expected. Not only am I headlining MonsterMadness, which was a given, but I get to win against Iris. How perfect. Maybe it will finally put that impossible harpy in her place.

I did my best to hide my gleeful smile behind my glass as Charlie and I toasted the news. He may be an old family friend, but he doesn't need to know I look forward to beating Iris in front of the entire EMW fan base. That would just be flat-out unprofessional.

The only downside to this whole thing is that now I have to train with the harpy. I would love to avoid her as much as possible, but Charlie is right. It's been too long since we were in a match together. And as much as I don't like Iris, I don't want to injure her.

I should honestly go back to my hotel room and get some rest since Iris and I are expected to start training together tomorrow, but I need a drink and some time with my girls. Navigating the halls, I find my way back to the locker room where Gianna stands behind a sitting June, combing the dragon's freshly washed golden mane.

"Hey!" I begin, and they both look at me. "Would you two want to get a drink or two? I heard there's a decent pub down the street with local brews on tap and amazing fried pickles. You in?"

Gianna's wolven ears perk toward me. "As long as there's something cheesy and fried."

"Agreed!" June licks her lips. "Fighting Iris is fun but always a lot of work."

"Ugh!" I groan. "Fuck Iris."

Gianna and June glance at each other before looking back at me.

"What did she do *this* time?" June asks with a sigh and a roll of her eyes.

"Just being a bitch, as usual." I look around the locker room, making sure it's just me and my friends. "Charlie told me that I'm taking her on at MonsterMadness."

Gianna's ears perk up. "Are you main eventing?"

"Of course I'm main eventing." I puff out my chest. "I *am* the reigning champion."

"Are you winning?"

"Duh!"

June sucks in a breath. "Oh. I bet Iris is pissed."

"I don't care how she feels. What sucks is that I have to start training with her tomorrow when we get back to Metroville." I clench my teeth.

"Seriously?" June's nose crinkles "But that means you don't get a day off."

"Is that what you took away from this? I don't care about the day off." I cross my arms over my chest. "I've been working every day since I was a calf. It's the fact I have to train with her."

June shrugs. "Iris isn't that bad. She's actually super great to train with."

"Easy for you to say. She doesn't *hate* you."

"Sure," Gianna interjects, fluffing June's mane. "But she's a professional. Just be cool, and she'll be cool."

"Why do *I* have to be the bigger monster here?"

"Someone has to be." Gianna sighs. "And it might as well be you."

"Whatever," I grumble. "Let me change into some street clothes so we can go to the pub."

I love my friends, but it annoys me that they don't understand my issue with Iris. They weren't there the first time I met the harpy, and I'll never forget the way she looked at me with such contempt, as if I were a stain on her favorite blouse.

Charlie was so excited to introduce us, claiming that Iris was the next great wrestler of our generation. It was intimidating talk, especially on my first day of developmental training with the EMW. Sure, I had trained under my father for years but never in any official capacity.

The harpy's ethereal beauty stunned me. Her massive wings caught my attention first, extraordinary with their gray patterned feathers that looked positively silky to the touch. They flexed when she looked at me, the muscles of her lithe frame tensing with the movement.

Her dark-gray hair was plaited into two long braids, giving me an unobstructed view of her sharp yet beautiful features. But it was her piercing violet eyes that took my breath away. To this day, I'm still not sure if they are actually the color of wisteria or if the light gray of her skin and down feathers makes them seem more vibrant.

It's embarrassing to admit that when Charlie finished introductions, I just stared at Iris, too blown away by her beauty to say anything. When she held out her hand to shake mine, all I could manage was a snort and a smile, hoping it was enough of a greeting.

What would I have said to her? *Hello? You are the most beautiful creature I've ever seen. Why don't you sit on my face?* No way.

And I knew I had made the right call when she glared at me like she'd just swallowed a lemon but was trying to play it cool. How would she have reacted if Charlie hadn't been there?

Ever since then, she's treated me like garbage. I get that it was rude not to shake her hand, but I smiled. That should be enough. And it certainly didn't warrant her scornful behavior that still plagues me to this day.

I used to wonder if she was jealous, but honestly she shouldn't be. Though I hate to admit it, Iris is a fantastic heel and gets plenty of airtime, so I have no idea what her problem is.

Shaking myself from that memory, I change into more casual clothing: low-waisted jeans and a crop top made from one of my official EMW shirts. Some may say it's tacky to wear your own face on a shirt, but I don't care. I look as cute as fuck.

"Oh, my goddess, Lena!" June eyes my ensemble. "Those jeans are really working for you."

I smirk. "I know. They really show off my abs, don't they?"

Gianna bites back a laugh. "Yeah. All eight of them," she teases.

"I could give you my routine, if you want."

"Nah!" Gianna pats her soft tummy. "My fans love my physique."

"What's that adorable nickname they have for you?" I ask with a smile.

"Luna Thicker." She fluffs her shiny black fur.

"It's perfect!" I boop her on the snout with my index finger. "Just like you."

And I mean it. I may be proud of my muscular build, but Gianna's soft and curvaceous figure is just as perfect. Every body in the EMW is valued and appreciated. All that matters is that you make wrestling look good.

"Hey!" June mock whines. "What about me?"

I pull the dragon into a hug. "You're perfect, too."

"Come on, Gi!" June beckons. "You know you want in on this."

Gianna turns up her nose. "I most certainly do not."

I laugh. "Quit lying to yourself and get in here."

The corners of her mouth lift in a small smile. "Fine. But only because you asked me to."

June and I open our arms, welcoming her into the fold. Gianna may appear prickly, but she's actually a big softie. When Gianna loves, she loves hard.

"Alright, alright," Gianna grumbles as her tail wags after a few long moments of hugging. "Can we finally go to the damn pub? I'm hungry as fuck."

"Better not let Gi get hangry." June snickers.

I smile softly at my friends. Where would I be without them? June and I became fast friends when Charlie decided we should tag team. But that's the thing about June: everyone is her friend. And I love that about her.

When Gi joined the EMW, her gruff exterior made it hard for me to attempt a friendship, but June's sunny disposition eventually dissipated the storm cloud always hanging above the wolven's head.

The best part about our friendship is that Charlie wrote it into our storyline as well, so that the three of us could go out in public together. I have friends who play heels, but with the EMW forcing us to stay in character for the general public, we have to play the part both on-screen and off. It sucks that I can't spend time with them in public outside of work, but at least I have June and Gianna.

The good news about having a fully serviceable locker room at whatever venue we perform is that it gives us time to freshen up without having to fight through a sea of fans to get back to our hotel rooms. For one, as babyfaces, we're supposed to be nice to fans, so it can take forever to get through unplanned public appearances. For another, I *hate* being photographed and not looking put together.

I'm the daughter of The Mighty Minos. I have a legacy to uphold. One I'm very proud to be a part of, even if it's sometimes exhausting.

We step into a nearly empty street that just an hour ago was teeming with EMW fans. "Let's go." I signal my friends to follow with a wave of my hand as I turn right. "The pub is about three blocks this way."

"That's not very far from here," Gianna observes. "Won't we run into fans?"

I shrug. "Who cares if we do?"

June skips ahead of me. "I don't! I love our fans! Maybe we'll even get free drinks!"

Gianna sighs. "Fine. I won't turn down a free drink or two."

The Water Cooler is dimly lit with scratched wooden floors, cracked cushions on large booths, and a few aging arcade machines. The walls are covered in a sea of Polaroids of various celebrities who have graced the humble establishment with their presence. I guess when the place is only a few blocks from the city's arena, it gets plenty of famous foot traffic.

We make it exactly five feet into the bar before we are greeted by a swarm of fans and their questions.

"Can you sign this for me?"

"Will you take a picture with me?"

"Is wrestling fake?"

My friends and I do our best to sign and take photos but ignore the questions about the industry's validity. I hate when we're asked if what we do is fake. The bumps we take and the stunts we do are very real. Wrestling is definitely scripted, but our athleticism is not a fraud.

"Alright, alright!" A burly security orc pushes his way through the crowd. "That's enough!"

We're ushered to a large corner booth, and cold, frothy beers are placed in our hands by a mothperson wearing a shirt with the pub's logo across the chest.

"Sorry about that." He offers us a genuine smile. "I'm Danny, the owner of this fine establishment, and we're delighted you're here. What can I get for ya?"

"Thank the goddess!" June lets out a sigh, slumping into the booth. "We're super hungry. Can we get every appetizer you have?"

Danny's laugh is hearty. "Coming right up. Our fried pickles are famous."

I beam. "That's exactly why we came here. That and the local brews."

"You won't be disappointed, Ms. Stronghorn."

"Please, call me Helen."

"I'll be out shortly with your food. Thank you so much, Helen." He takes a few steps toward the kitchen before pausing and turning back to look at us. "Oh. I hope you don't mind, but some of your coworkers are already here. I know you aren't on the best of terms."

Danny motions toward a booth on the opposite side of the pub. Pan, Daphne, and, unfortunately, Iris sit huddled together over a plate of nachos. The demon and the satyr offer us tiny, discreet smiles while the harpy stares me down. Even from across the room, the venom in her glare is obvious.

I roll my eyes at her. She can glower at me all she wants; I'm not letting her get to me.

Not tonight. I'm turning over a new leaf. No more being bothered by Iris of the Harpy Clan.

That resolution lasts all of five seconds when Iris flips me the bird.

Oh, fuck her.

"Be the bigger person," Gianna mutters into my flicking ear. "And show her a little grace. She just found out she's losing at MonsterMadness."

"I don't get why she cares," I growl. "She's still getting the airtime."

Gianna sighs, rubbing her temples. "Sure. But winning MonsterMadness is a huge thing. Think about it. You're going to be an even bigger deal once you retain that title."

"It's not my fault she doesn't have the same star power as me."

June shakes her head. "Athena Rainstorm is one of our biggest draws. Didn't you hear the fans tonight?"

I cross my arms over my chest. June is right. Iris sells tickets. But there's no way you'll ever catch me admitting that out loud.

"Here you go!" Danny appears with a large tray, putting a pause on our conversation. I could kiss him right now.

June claps and giggles. "Thank you, Danny!" She snatches a mozzarella stick off the tray before the platter hits the table.

"Hot! Hot! Hot!" She gasps around a steaming bite, fanning her mouth.

Gianna scoffs. "You couldn't wait for it to cool?"

I pass the plate of chicken wings to the wolven. "Here. Eat these before you bite someone's head off."

She glares at me, but once she tears into a wing with her sharp canines, she closes her eyes and chews, looking as if she's having a pleasant dream. All my friends have food in their mouths. Good. Now it's my turn. I'm starving. Promos really work up my appetite.

I bite into a fried pickle spear, my eyes rolling back into my head. *Fuck.* They are super good, and the spicy sauce that comes with them is to die for.

My friends and I eat in silence for a few moments, enjoying the deliciously fried food and cold beers. We ignore the occasional stares of the pub patrons. My annoyance over having to train with Iris dissipates with each sip of my beverage.

It will all work out. Iris and I can be professionals. We'll put on a good show for our fans. MonsterMadness is the biggest event of the year. She surely wouldn't sabotage that just to get back at me for whatever perceived slight I've made against her.

"Oh!" June interrupts my train of thought. "A little update. I got an endorsement deal with Montu Sports."

I high-five her. "Hell yeah! What product are you promoting?"

June gushes about the company's latest athletic wear, and I settle into conversation with friends, happy to get my mind off Iris. By the time there's nothing but crumbs on the plate, the pub's crowd has thinned.

"Oh shit!" I look around for a clock. "What time is it?"

Gianna peers at the watch on her furry wrist. "Just a little after midnight."

"Fuck!" I hold up my hand to wave down Danny. "My flight leaves in a few hours. I should get some shut-eye."

"Not a bad idea." Gianna nods. "You also start training tomorrow."

"Ugh! Don't remind me."

June nudges me with her elbow. "Go ahead and get back to your hotel room. Gi and I can handle the check."

I press a hand over my heart as I offer her a small smile. "Thank you. That means a lot."

"No worries." She gives me a side hug. "What are friends for?"

I wiggle my way out of the booth and head toward the exit, glancing at the booth where Iris sat. She's not there anymore. Thank the goddess. I can't deal with her attitude anymore tonight.

There will be plenty of that tomorrow.

Commercial Break

Human Energy Drink

"Oh, goddess," the ghoul grumbles, resting his head on the desk. "I'm too tired. I shouldn't have stayed up so late last night watching wrestling."

The kraken sitting at the neighboring desk groans. "You're telling me! And coffee just isn't cutting it!"

"What are we going to do?" The ghoul tugs at his white hair. "The boss expects that report on her desk by the end of the day, and I just don't have the energy."

"I wish there was something to give us an extra boost!" The kraken sighs, rubbing her temples with two blue tentacles.

The cubicle walls crash around them. The two monsters slam backward, shoved by the sudden force. A large and beautiful minotaur dressed in a branded tank top and athletic pants steps onto the debris.

The kraken points at the intruder. "It's Helen Stronghorn!"

"The one and only!" The famous wrestler grins. "And I'm here to save the day!"

The ghoul's jaw drops. "But how?"

"Easy!" Helen produces a can of energy drink from behind her back. "With Human Energy Drink!"

"Human Energy Drink?" the office workers ask in unison.

Helen pops the tab, and the liquid fizzes out the top with a hiss. "The only energy drink that gives you the boost of a human accountant scurrying to reach a deadline at their nine-to-five!"

The two monsters look at each other, mouths agape.

"A human accountant?" asks the kraken. "That would solve all our problems!"

The minotaur tosses two cans of Human Energy Drink to them. "Drink up!"

The kraken and ghoul open their cans and tilt their heads back to gulp down the drinks.

"Wow!" the kraken jumps to a stand. "I feel like flying!"

The ghoul follows his coworker. "And I feel like finishing that report! Thank you, Helen Stronghorn!"

"No problem, tiny monsters!" Helen smiles down at the kraken and ghoul.

She turns to the camera, takes a long drink from the can, and flexes her sculpted biceps. "Human Energy Drink! Unleash your inner accountant!"

Chapter 5

Lena

What if I just called Charlie and told him that I'm sick? I'm so exhausted. The plane ride back to Metroville was too short to take a nap. How will I muster up the energy to face Iris?

But I don't really have a choice, so I grab a Human Energy Drink from the catering table in the EMW break room and chug it on my way to the locker room. I guess I'm as ready as I'll ever be to face my archnemesis. Both in the ring and out of it.

The gym is empty, which makes sense. We just performed last night. Why would anyone else be here? I love Charlie, but I can't help being annoyed by his request that I start training with Iris today. At least if other wrestlers were around, they could be a buffer, making Iris easier to deal with.

"What took you so long?"

I turn around to find Iris standing behind me, a scowl creasing her forehead. Of course she's going to rub in the fact that she got here first.

I scoff. "Can we at least try to be pleasant?"

"I can play nice when you start respecting my time."

"Fine. I'll try to be on time tomorrow," I grumble, rubbing my temples. This harpy is already giving me a headache.

"Try?" She ruffles her feathers. "Why don't you just be on time?"

"Listen closely, Iris." I jab a finger toward her face, my tail swishing furiously. "You're lucky I'm even here right now."

She rolls her eyes. "That's right. I forgot I'm in the presence of the *great* Helen Stronghorn. I should be on my hands and knees thanking you for gracing me with your presence."

I force a smirk. "It would be a start." But something about the way she said my name in such a mocking tone hurts.

Iris opens her mouth to say something back but is interrupted by the cerberus Lucy, EMW's head trainer. "Alright, ladies. That's enough."

We jolt apart. Lucy may be short, but she's tenacious and not someone you want to mess with.

"She started it," I growl.

All three of Lucy's brindle heads sigh. "Why did Charles assign me to train you two knuckleheads?" asks her middle head, which usually does most of the talking.

"Knuckleheads?" Iris flaps her wings.

Lucy's left head bares her fangs while her middle head frowns. "Yes. That's what you'll be until you two can learn to get along."

"Try to be a bit nicer," her right head urges. "It's hard working together when you hate each other."

Her middle head's nostrils flare. "Don't coddle them! They need to learn to be professionals."

I bite back a retort. There's no point getting pissy with Lucy. She's only here to help, which I desperately hope she can.

All three of the trainer's heads look between us, daring us to sass back. They smile when we remain silent.

"Excellent." She claps her hands. "Let's get started. Mr. Palmer mentioned he wants to see a suplex from the top rope at some point."

"From the top rope?" Iris and I echo at the same time, mouths agape.

We're going to have to practice to make sure we get this right. A suplex from the top rope can easily result in injury for both parties if we aren't careful, especially with our size difference. It's something both of us are capable of, being the experienced wrestlers that we are, but part of our job is learning how to be safe.

"Yes. So maybe we should practice suplexing from the mat before going to the top rope."

"Wait!" Iris gives the hand signal for a time out. "Who is suplexing who?"

Lucy chews her bottom lip, glancing between me and Iris. "Iris will be suplexing Lena."

"What?" I clench my fists.

Me? Getting suplexed from the top rope? You've got to be fucking kidding me!

Iris's eyes sparkle as she grins. Of course she's smiling. She doesn't have to be on the receiving end of the stunt.

Lucy holds up her hands. "Don't worry, Lena. While the crowd will be impressed by Athena suplexing Helen, they'll be even more impressed when you walk away from it unharmed before executing your finisher."

The harpy's expression sours. Now it's my turn to smile. I hate that I, Helen "Mother" Stronghorn, will be suplexed off the top rope, but I guess it will be pretty cool to recover from it and still win the match. Especially at Iris's expense.

"Let's head to the mats." Lucy waves for us to come along with her.

Iris and I narrow our eyes at each other one last time before following our trainer. We step onto the crash mats and await Lucy's instructions, standing at least six feet apart, neither one of us wanting to get close to the other.

"Alright." Lucy looks between us. "I hate to break it to you two, but you're going to have to touch each other."

With a sigh, Iris steps forward. At six and a half feet tall, I tower over most of my opponents, and Iris is no exception. At five and a half feet, she's kind of short for a monster wrestler, but it doesn't stop her from being a commanding presence in the ring.

I turn around, back facing Iris, so I'm in the ideal position to be suplexed.

"Don't just stand there," Lucy's right head urges. "Lift Lena and suplex her. And Lena, I want Iris to understand how to lift someone of your size and stature without assistance, so no helping her, alright?"

"Fine," Iris mutters before wrapping her arms around my hips.

With a grunt, she attempts to lift me, but our height difference prevents her from getting my hooves off the ground.

"Try again," Lucy encourages. "Lift with your legs."

Iris attempts lifting me for a second time but lets out a groan of frustration when she fails again.

Ha! Maybe I won't have to deal with a suplex after all.

Lucy rubs her middle chin. "You may have to give your wings a flap or two to get Lena off the mat."

I can't help but sneer. "Poor tiny Iris. Unable to lift me. How embarrassing."

With a shriek, she flaps her wings, taking me to the sky with her. I look down, horrified that we are at least six feet above the top rope of the ring next to us. My heart pounds, and I break out into a cold sweat. That's a long way down, and I don't like it one bit.

Oh shit. Maybe it was a bad idea to taunt her.

My stomach swoops as she dives back toward the ground. My face is going to hit first. I screw my eyes shut, bracing myself. This is going to hurt even if I'm landing on a crash mat.

But at the last moment, she opens her wings, slowing our descent at a mere foot above the ground. With a smirk, she plops me onto the mat, the soft material cushioning the short fall.

Oh, fuck this bitch!

With a roar, I shove myself to standing. "What the fuck? You could have hurt me!"

Iris clutches her stomach as she laughs. "But I didn't. You should have seen your face."

"Fuck you!" I spit.

"Awh." She mock pouts. "Did the big, bad Helen Stronghorn get scared?"

I grab her by the shirt collar. "Never do that again!"

"Or what?" A challenge burns in her eyes.

"What the hell is going on here?" a thick Texan accent calls out from across the gym.

Thank the goddess. Charlie will put the harpy in her place. Iris stiffens and her lips press into a thin line. Letting go of her shirt, I take a step back, placing my hands on my hips. I can't wait for Charlie to lay into her.

"Lena." Charlie tuts as he approaches. "I expected better of you."

I gape at him. What? Am I really getting scolded right now?

"But Charlie, she—"

He holds up his hand to silence me. "I don't want to hear it. I expected this kind of behavior from Miss Iris, but not my leading lady."

Iris schools her features, but she can't hide her left eye twitching. She's pissed. I can see why. Charlie's words are a tad harsh. I would feel kind of bad for her if she hadn't risked injuring me with that stupid little stunt she just pulled.

Charlie settles his disapproving gaze onto Iris. "I assume you haven't changed your mind about main eventing MonsterMadness?"

She shakes her head. "No, sir."

"Then you need to start acting like it." He turns to Zach, his grimy human assistant. "Write this down."

Zach scrambles to open the notebook he clutches against his chest. "What do you need, sir?"

"Note that I counseled Miss Iris and Lena on their behavior and mandated off-hours bonding experiences."

My heart feels stuck in my throat as the assistant scribbles Charlie's words. Excuse me? What does that even mean?

"Charlie?" I say his name tentatively. "Are you suggesting we spend *more* time together?"

His eyes narrow, assessing me. "I am, Lena. If you two can't even be civil long enough to practice a move, how will you plan a whole match?" Charlie cocks his head. "Do you have a problem with that?"

Shit. Charlie may be a family friend, but he's still my boss. I must be careful with how I proceed.

I shake my head. "No. I'm just not sure how we can accomplish that."

Iris continues to stare, mouth agape. She's obviously too stunned to back me up against this ludicrous idea.

"I don't hire idiots. Figure it out." He twirls his mustache between his fingers for a moment, as if deep in thought. "But since I'm feeling generous today, I'll give you an idea. Maybe start with having a meal together. Not in public, mind you."

Eating with Iris? But I love food! And I definitely don't want her bad attitude souring a perfectly good meal.

I open my mouth to protest, but Iris finally decides to speak up. "Whatever you say, sir."

That bitch! I clench my fists, nails digging into my palms. We might have been able to get out of this if we'd both protested.

Charlie claps her on the shoulder. "That's what I like to hear." He tips his hat to us. "Now, if you'll excuse me."

I watch in disbelief as Charlie saunters out of the gym. Did that really happen? Why didn't I fight harder against this stupid plan?

Oh yeah. Iris agreed to this shit.

I turn to the harpy, nostrils flaring. "What the fuck was that?"

She scowls. "You act like we had a choice."

"We did! We could have fought him on this."

She jabs a finger to my chest. "Maybe *you* could. You're guaranteed to main event MonsterMadness no matter what. But I can't afford to lose this opportunity."

Oh. I deflate at her confession. As much as I would love to wrestle literally *anyone* else, I'm not going to be a total asshat and sabotage this for her. It's every wrestler's dream to main event MonsterMadness. Besides, out of the entire roster, no one deserves this opportunity more than her. Except me.

And while Charlie might not take my spot at MonsterMadness away, he could tell my dad that I'm not cooperating. Disappointing my father is not something I want to do. I have a legacy to uphold, and I can't do that by being difficult and bratty. My dad may have taught me to take what I want, whenever I want, but he also taught me to respect our reputation.

My ears twitch as I stand up tall, determined to figure out a way to make this work for the both of us. "Fine. When should we have dinner together?"

Iris's smile is soft and genuine. She's never looked at me like this before. I can't help but grin back at her.

Maybe this whole arrangement won't be so bad.

As if remembering who she's talking to, Iris's eyes narrow into her signature glare.

I sweep my arms wide, my tail flicking. "What did I say *this* time?"

"Just because we have to do this doesn't mean I want to."

"And you think I'm jumping at the chance to hang out with you?" I scoff. "Get a clue."

Her cheeks darken to a deep-blue gray. She opens her mouth to retort when Lucy steps in between us, saving the day yet again.

"Alright, ladies. Why don't each of you do some strength training? Separately. Get your emotions under control before you make dinner plans."

"Fine," Iris huffs, glowering at me one last time before heading toward the weight room.

Lucy rubs the temples on her middle head while the other two let out deep sighs. "I need a raise."

I pat Lucy's shoulder. "I wish she would apologize for her behavior, but I swear she'll never learn."

"You think this is all on her?" Lucy snaps. "Take a long look in the mirror, Lena. But first, dead lifts." She stomps her foot and points toward the weight room. "I'll be in to check on you two in a few moments. Please don't kill each other before I get back."

"I can't make any promises."

Lucy shoots me a rude hand gesture while all three of her heads stare daggers at me.

I guess I deserved that.

Chapter 6

Iris

"Ugh! You just don't get it." I grumble to Pan and Daphne over a bottle of wine at my cozy, high-rise studio apartment.

I love my place, with its large windows, plush sofa, and local art adorning the lavender walls. Nothing compares to coming home after traveling for a match and throwing myself on my massive bed with sheets in the highest thread count money can buy. My apartment may not be as big as the others in my complex, but I don't need much space. I just want somewhere I can be me.

"We get it!" Daphne groans. "You hate Lena. What's new?"

Pan runs a finger along the edge of their wineglass, tilting their horned head. "It's probably not too late to back out of the main eventing."

I wrinkle my nose. "Hell, no!"

They shrug. "Then you're going to have to deal with it."

Daphne titters, twirling a beaded braid in her fingers. "You know what would really help?"

Pan and I stare at her, waiting for the answer.

"If you two just fucked already."

"Excuse me?" I gag. Sleeping with Lena? No, thank you.

Pan nods, rubbing their chin. "Hmmm…"

My gaze darts between my friends. "You can't be serious."

"It might open up the doorway to communication," Pan says.

I quirk a brow. "Umm…how?"

Daphne clicks her tongue. "When was the last time you got laid?"

"I don't see why that matters."

"Orgasms are the great equalizer. They make you all relaxed and gooey. And if you give them to each other, it will relieve a lot of tension and make you more receptive."

Pan tops off our glasses, the red liquid the same color as their skin. "I may have never given anyone an orgasm, but I know how I feel after I give myself one. I could negotiate world peace."

Daphne ribs Pan with an elbow. "You've been the cause of plenty of orgasms. They don't call you 'The Temptation' for nothing."

Their cheeks darken, and they look away, focusing instead on their wineglass.

I grimace. Daphne means well, but Pan is so shy it's almost painful. But it's not just about their social life, but their romantic life as well. They have plenty of prospects. Both EMW fans and nonfans alike know of their ethereal beauty. It just takes a lot to get them out of their shell, and, unfortunately, they haven't found someone willing to be patient enough to coax them out of it.

"Well." I clear my throat. "I am *not* fucking Lena of the Minotaur Clan."

Pan looks at me, eyes softening, no doubt grateful to refocus the conversation back on me.

Daphne rolls her eyes. "You're no fun."

"Why don't *you* sleep with her, then?" I ask with a smug grin.

"Lena may be fine as hell, but I have plenty of tasty morsels in my roster." Daphne shrugs. "Besides, I wouldn't dare come between two monsters so obviously destined to be together."

I snort. "What are you talking about?"

"Oh, come on. Have you never noticed the chemistry between you two?"

"I can't stand Lena!" I ruffle my feathers. "How could there be chemistry between us?"

Pan runs a hand through the silky tresses of their bob. "Daphne is right. I honestly can't wait to see how well you perform together during MonsterMadness. The crowd will go nuts!"

I cross my arms over my chest. "Did you not hear the part where I said I can't stand her?"

Daphne waves me off. "Yeah, yeah. You think she grew up with a silver spoon in her mouth. Blah. Blah. Blah. Did you not pay attention to how hard she works? She may be a nepotism baby, but she doesn't act like one."

"Excuse me?" I wave my hands in the air. "What about her massive ego?"

Daphne shrugs. "And you don't have one? You can't be a performer without a bit of an ego."

My wings droop. I'm so over this conversation.

Pan clears their throat. "When is your first dinner together?"

"Tomorrow. And I'm the one hosting."

"That's good." Pan nods. "Gives you an advantage; you'll likely be more comfortable."

"True." I rub my chin. "I hadn't thought of it that way."

Pan has a point. Originally, I was upset that Lena would come barreling into my safe space and ruin it. But now that I think about it, it puts her in an awkward position, not me.

"What are you cooking?" Pan asks.

Daphne laughs. "Iris? Cook? Be serious."

I glare at my friend. "I can cook!"

Her gaze softens. "I love you, babe. You know that. But when was the last time you used that kitchen for anything more than storing wine and ice cream?"

"Hey!" I bring my hand to my chest. "I'll have you know I use the toaster for my Pop-Tarts."

"Great!" She rolls her eyes. "Which flavor will you serve Lena? Brown Sugar or Wild Berry?"

I stick my tongue out. "You know Brown Sugar is the worst one."

Daphne smirks. "So Wild Berry?"

"I'm not serving Pop-Tarts." I rub my temples as my wings droop. "I need to figure out where to order takeout from. It has to be really good. I don't want to give Lena any more ammunition to be a bitch to me."

Pan flicks their wrist to look at their watch. “I don’t mean to be rude, but I really should be getting home. I want to get to the gym early and get my workout in before everyone else shows up.”

“No worries. Anything in particular that you’re training for?” I smile at them as I stand. The room spins, and I fight the urge to sit back down. Am I drunk?

“Uh…” Pan holds out a hand to steady me. “How much did you have to drink?”

“As much as you did…I think.”

Pan chortles. “Let’s get you to bed.”

“No, no.” I take their empty wineglass. “I’m fine. It was just a little head rush. What was I saying? Oh yeah. What are you training for?”

They hold my gaze as if unsure if they want to believe me or not. After a few moments, they smile. “I have a rematch against Gianna, and I’m scripted to win this time. I want my finishing move to be extra impressive.”

“What move are you going to do?”

“You’ll have to wait and see.” Pan winks.

Daphne rises from the sofa. “You know Pan likes to surprise everyone, including us.”

She hands me her wineglass. “I should probably get going, too.”

I furrow my brows. “Are you both okay to walk home? Should I call a cab?”

Pan offers me a relieved smile. “That would be great, thank you.”

“Oh!” Daphne’s goat-like ears perk up. “Can we share?”

“Of course.”

I make quick work of ordering their ride before escorting them, with both Pan and Daphne’s cloven hooves clacking on the tile floors, to the front lobby of my complex. It’s not long before the cab rolls up. With quick hugs and air-kisses, I bid my friends farewell.

Once they are safely in the cab, I make my way back to the elevator. I giggle as I sway on my taloned feet, staring at the buttons. Why are they blurring together? Silly buttons. They should just stay still for a second.

Once I succeed in pressing the correct button, I cling to the side of the elevator the entire ride to my floor and contemplate the day’s events. Maybe I shouldn't have scared Lena today, but I saw red as soon as she started mocking me. She knows I'm strong enough to lift her, so her comment was uncalled for and only meant to piss me off.

What's upsetting is that she succeeded. I shouldn't let her get to me. But it's hard not to when she sounds so smug. That 'I'm better than you' tone makes me fly into a blind rage every time she addresses me.

But I need to learn to keep my cool in her presence. Being a star in the EMW is something I have dreamt about since I was a kid. I used to glue myself to the television, sitting as close as my parents would let me before they scolded me to move back. Of course my hero was The Mighty Minos. He was literally the coolest.

I wanted nothing more than to hoist that EMW Realms Championship belt above my head as the crowd cheered for me, elated by my victory. But I'm starting to think that will never happen. Who wants to see the most hated heel in the company win the championship?

It was too easy to cast me as a heel. Being a member of the Harpy Clan means I grew up surrounded by powerful females, never afraid to speak their minds and take what they wanted. It gave me a good blueprint for taking on the role of the overly confident and snarky harpy.

My dreams feel further and further away with each turn of my storyline. Main eventing MonsterMadness should be good enough for me. I'll be the second biggest star in the EMW. But fuck if I don't want my childhood dream to come true. Even if the matches are predetermined, it matters to that child inside me who still yearns for it.

Instead, Lena gets to live my dream life. A life she was handed because of her famous dad. While I still adore The Mighty Minos, there's a small part of me that resents him for raising such an entitled daughter. How much of a role did he play in her turning out to be such a brat?

The door to my apartment slams closed behind me as I stumble past the table my where my phone sits. I pause to eye the crumpled piece of paper next to the receiver. Lena's number. She gave it to me so I could call her tomorrow with directions to my place.

I wish our magic didn't make it impossible for the monster realm to have cell phones like the human realm does. It'd be so much more convenient to just give her my address and hope her GPS could navigate to my apartment. But no. Instead, I have to call her and walk her through directions.

Wait a second. I have Lena's number.

A wicked smile curls my lips as I reach for the receiver. I know exactly how to get back at her.

It takes me a few tries, but I finally manage to punch her number into the dial pad, attempting to stifle my laughter with a hand over my mouth. After three rings, the hesitant voice of Lena picks up.

"Hello?"

"Good evening, ma'am. This is a routine call from…uhh…the electric company. We have a couple of quick questions. First, we need to know, is your refrigerator running?"

Lena lets out a deep sigh. "Yes, it's running and no, I'm not going to go catch it. What the fuck, Iris? Why are you prank calling me? Do you know what time it is?"

I stiffen. "This isn't Iris. This is the electric company."

"Come on. You think I don't recognize your voice?"

Oh.

She groans. "Are you drunk or something?"

"Maybe a little." I blush when I realize that the response came out slurred.

"Go to bed."

"Wait!" I listen. There's no dial tone. Good. That means she hasn't hung up on me yet. "Why are you such a brat?"

"Did you really call me at ten at night to insult me?"

"Are you going to answer the question?" I ask with a shrill titter.

"Goodnight, Iris. I'll call back tomorrow to get directions to your place."

A click followed by a dial tone. Ha! She hung up! I'll mark that as a point for me.

Feeling smug, I begin my bedtime routine. It may be a little sloppy, but I would never go to bed without completing it. Teeth brushing, skin care, slipping into silk pajamas, and finally twisting my hair into two long braids. But by the time I finally lie down in my bed, my victory tastes less sweet.

I embarrassed myself. Drunk dialing my rival? How juvenile of me. And what if she decides to tell Charles? I would be screwed. But she didn't say she would tell him. So maybe I'm safe? I'll just have to apologize first thing tomorrow morning.

Lucy gave us the day off from training, so we aren't forced into a potentially heated situation. She wants us to spend some time together outside of work first, in the hopes that we bond and find common ground. I doubt that will happen, but those are her orders. That gives me plenty of time to figure out what to order before Lena comes over for dinner.

Pizza? No. Too casual.

Sushi? Hmm...that could work. There's an amazing sushi spot a few blocks away. But which rolls do I order?

But I don't dwell on this long. The wine, coupled with the emotional and physical exhaustion from my confrontation with Lena today, help me slip into a dreamless sleep.

Commercial Break

The Puppysitter

An ogre in a professionally tailored suit knocks on the front door of a cabin in the middle of the woods. Luna Thrasher answers with a yawn, her usually perfect waves a tangled mess and her black fur ruffled.

"Can I help you?"

The scene cuts to the ogre and Luna sitting at a table in a kitchen decorated with roosters. Luna clutches a piece of paper, her hands trembling.

"Unless you can come up with the money in three months' time," the ogre warns, "your grandmother's land belongs to the city. They have big plans for the space—a mega mall."

"But that's impossible!" Luna whines. "How will I come up with the money? I don't make enough at the EMW to pay for this!"

A deep and distinctive voice narrates over the footage of Luna crying alone at the table while looking at the paperwork. *"What will this down-on-her-luck wolven megastar do to save her ancestral home?"*

A quick transition shows Luna browsing the Help Wanted ads in the newspaper. The camera zooms in on a position for a nanny.

"She might just have to start moonlighting in puppy care," announces the narrator.

The next shot shows Luna sitting in an ornately decorated sitting room facing two gray wolvens.

"Why would an EMW wrestler want to be a nanny?" asks the female wolven, clutching her expensive pearl necklace.

The male wolven shrugs. "I say we give her a chance, honey. Who knows? She might be able to protect our little angel better than your typical nanny."

Luna lets out a sigh of relief. "Great! When do I get to meet the kid?"

A piercing howl echoes through the house, followed by a flurry of footsteps. With a big leap, a gray wolven puppy bursts into the sitting room, her tail wagging.

"Is this my new nanny?" The puppy bombards her parents with questions. "When do we get to play? Does she like fetch?"

Her father pats her head, while her mother explains, "We've had difficulty keeping nannies for our Angelica in the past. They never last longer than a month. I guess we keep hiring flakes. If you can stay on for the next three months, we'll have a nice bonus check for you."

The camera zooms on Luna's smiling face. "No problem."

She glances at Angelica, and the camera cuts to the puppy. She glares daggers at Luna while gesturing the universal sign for *I'm watching you* with her fingers.

Luna's smile falters as she audibly gulps.

"Luna 'The Alpha' Thrasher stars in this feel-good comedy that will get the whole family's tails wagging," declares the narrator over footage of Angelica laying out a trap with a bucket perched on the top of the door and marbles scattered on the ground.

The scene cuts to Luna walking through the door, only to have the bucket fall on her head. She then slips on the marbles and falls in a loud crash. Angelica laughs hysterically, clutching her belly.

"You little punk!" growls Luna, and she chases the puppy throughout the house.

The narrator cuts in over footage of Luna and Angelica glaring at each other. *"See* The Puppysitter *in a theater near you on Winter Solstice Day."*

The footage fades, and the movie logo on top of the release date fills the screen. The narrator's voice returns one last time.

"You're guaranteed to have a howling good time."

Chapter 7

Lena

I BRACE MYSELF AS I knock on Iris's door. It will be okay. I can sit through dinner. How long will it even take? No more than thirty minutes, right? Fingers crossed, I can get in and out and back to my life.

Iris answers the door dressed in baggy sweatpants and an oversized EMW shirt from my father's generation. Her hair is pulled up in a messy bun. If not for her signature scowl and mesmerizing violet eyes, I would have wondered if I was at the right apartment. Iris is always so put together. It's weird seeing her dressed down.

"Are you going to just stand there, or are you coming in?" she asks with a grumble and snap of her wings.

Great. Here we go.

"I just didn't recognize you at first," I say through the gritted teeth of a forced smile.

Her eyes narrow. "What is that supposed to mean?"

I sigh. "Why is everything a fight with you?"

She opens her mouth but then closes it. Iris considers me with a frown before shaking her head. "Come in."

Wow. That's surprising. I expected her to bite my head off, but I'll accept this olive branch, no matter how small.

When I step into Iris's apartment and look around, I'm stunned once again. I don't know what I was expecting, but it certainly wasn't a cozy studio apartment decked out in colorful art. Based on her cold exterior, I always imagined her home would be just as sterile and uninviting.

"Welcome." Iris sweeps a hand through the air. "Would you like anything to drink?"

"Uh…" My eyes land on a large poster of my father hanging on the wall next to her bed. Alright. So Iris is definitely an old-school wrestling fan and, in particular, of my dad.

Many contemporary wrestlers grew up watching The Mighty Minos. As a result, they all usually treat me like some sort of royalty. But not Iris. She hates me despite idolizing my father. Something unfamiliar flutters in my chest.

"Are you okay?"

Iris's question interrupts my thoughts.

"Yes." I clear my throat, refocusing my attention. "Sorry. I'll take room temperature water."

She stares at me, blinking rapidly. "I wasn't prepared for that. I have water from the filter. It's chilled. Unless you want tap water."

"I'll take the filtered water, thanks." I hate cold water, but I refuse to drink tap. I'll suck it up. Besides, it's not like I have to be here too long.

"I also have hot green tea," Iris offers as she makes me a glass of water with no ice.

"What are we having for dinner?"

She nods her head toward a large brown paper bag. "I ordered sushi."

I hide my grimace. "Green tea would be great, then. Thanks."

Ugh. Iris ordered takeout? Can she not cook? It's not like Metroville is a bad food city or anything, but I must admit I'm spoiled by my own cooking. Maybe it's for the best that I'm not getting a home-cooked meal from Iris. It's harder for her to poison me this way.

After serving me a mug of steaming tea, Iris pulls two plates and sauce cups out of her cupboards, handing me a set without saying a word. "I wasn't sure what kind of sushi you like, so I grabbed one of each specialty roll."

"But that's so much food!"

"I didn't want to mess this up," she admits as she unpacks the bag, displaying the various sushi rolls on the kitchen island.

"What do you mean?" I ask, grabbing the closest roll piled high with crabmeat.

Iris's cheeks flush. "I shouldn't have drunk dialed you last night. That wasn't cool. And…I'm sorry. I'm trying to make up for it now by making sure you have sushi that you like."

"Did you just apologize?" I ask, giving her a double take.

"I did." She turns away from me, her chin in the air. "Don't get used to it."

I hold back a laugh. Iris of the Harpy Clan actually apologized to me? I'll take it. "Thank you."

She hands me a pair of chopsticks without a word and then begins dishing a variety of sushi onto her plate. I wait for her to say more, but when she doesn't, I follow her lead, piling my plate high with food. When I take my first bite, I hold back a groan of satisfaction. The food is fantastic. Iris knows how to pick a good sushi place.

I consider extending my own olive branch and telling her this, but when I glance in her direction, I change my mind. She glares down at her plate as she shoves bite after bite into her mouth in a quiet fury.

Never mind. If she wants to sit there and sulk like a brat, I don't really want to talk to her anyway.

So, Iris and I stand over her kitchen island, only the sound of our chewing to break the silence. Couldn't she have at least put on some music? We don't even look at each other, choosing to glare at our plates instead.

"I'm done," I declare once I've eaten my fill which, thankfully, didn't take long.

Iris finally fixes her violet eyes on me. "Did you save room for dessert?"

I blink at her. "You didn't tell me there was any. I can't eat another bite."

She puts her hands on her hips. "How can you eat dinner without having something sweet after?"

"Because I'm not eight years old."

Iris gasps. "You don't have to be a child to enjoy dessert!"

"Maybe not, but what kind of adult has a sweet tooth like that? I also have a figure to maintain. You don't get to be the great Helen Stronghorn by eating sweets every night."

She clenches her jaw. "Why do you always have to insult everyone?"

I stand tall, squaring my shoulders. "I don't insult everyone!"

"Yes, you do. Since the day you started at the EMW, you've been nothing but a spoiled wretch."

I cross my arms over my chest. "You've got to be fucking kidding me. Give me one example."

"Easy. The time you screamed at that poor werecat for not getting your perfect curls bouncy enough."

Werecat? What the hell is she talking about? I do my best to recall my interactions with werecats, but I come up blank.

"You don't even remember, do you?" Iris huffs. "Her name is Mindy, if that helps."

Oh! Mindy! I do remember Mindy and the incident Iris is referring to. Mindy is a great hair and makeup artist, but she did mess up that one time. And I didn't scream at her. I think? Besides, there hasn't been any faux pas since, so maybe she needed a good scolding.

"You don't get it." I wave a hand over my hair and face. "I have an image to uphold. My curls are my signature."

"Doesn't give you an excuse to go off on the poor girl. You made her cry, you know."

I pause. Is that true? Did I really make Mindy cry? I didn't mean to. The pressure to be perfect is so overwhelming that I sometimes lash out, but I never intend to hurt anyone. Not that Iris would ever understand. She didn't grow up like I did. No one could ever understand how it feels to get a call from their father chastising them about how the chaps they wore weren't sparkly enough.

"Whatever." I sniff, choosing not to address how awful I feel about the werecat. "That's only one instance, and I'll apologize the next time I see her. This doesn't really prove your point."

"You snubbed me the first time we met." Iris scowls. "Couldn't even bother to shake my hand."

My tail flicks in annoyance. "Are you serious? You hate me over a handshake? That's quite petty, if you ask me."

"I have a laundry list of reasons to hate you." She flexes her wings.

"Oh yeah?" I gesture *come on* with my hands. "Let's hear them."

Iris glances at the clock on the wall. "I would need a whole day to go through all your flaws, but I actually want to get some sleep tomorrow before we have to be back at the gym."

"You're pathetic," I growl.

"You just can't handle someone putting you in your place," she says as she clears my plate from the countertop.

I shake my head. This entire interaction is so pointless. What am I even doing here? "You're impossible."

Iris glowers at me, violet eyes full of fire. "It's probably best if you leave now."

"Fine." I stomp toward the door.

"Wait!"

"Yes?" I pause, a smirk forming on my lips, ready for the second apology of the night.

"Don't forget your dessert," she sneers, tossing me a cardboard container that I barely manage to catch. "It's a slice of matcha cake."

My entire face and neck heat up. The audacity of this bitch.

Instead of dropping the cake on the ground and smashing it with my hoof like I should, I clutch it to my chest and step out of the apartment. No point in wasting a perfectly good slice of cake.

When I step into the gym the next morning, over a half hour early for my scheduled training session, I partially expect Iris to already be there, ready to mock me for 'being late.' But it's just Lucy waiting for me.

"Oh! You're here early," she says, all three heads smiling at me.

"Where's Iris?"

The eyes of her middle head roll. "Good morning to you, too."

I rub my temples. "Sorry. Dinner didn't go well last night, so I'm not exactly looking forward to seeing her today."

"Good thing I staggered your training time, then."

"You did?" I ask, perking up. "So, I don't have to deal with her?"

"Nope," Lucy answers with a pop of her lips. "I figured it would be a good idea to give you two a few days of mandated bonding time before you started working together again."

"Honestly, I would prefer just to train with her and get it over with."

She shrugs. "Mr. Palmer's orders. You can take it up with him if you don't like it."

"Now, Lena," drawls Charlie, appearing at the doorway of the gym, "what don't you like?"

How does that man always show up at the most inconvenient times?

I screw my eyes shut and inhale a deep breath. *Don't screw this up.* "I was thinking it might be more beneficial if Iris and I just rehearse rather than spend all of this time together after hours."

He cocks his head, stroking his mustache. "And why is that?"

"Because the time could be better used. Maybe by promoting MonsterMadness or solo training."

If I didn't know Charles Palmer, I might call the smile he gives me empathetic and think he understands where I'm coming from. I would be wrong. The smile on Charlie's face says one thing and one thing only: I am in trouble.

"Interesting idea, Lena." He twirls his mustache between his forefinger and thumb. "I'll give it some thought."

That's Charlie's way of telling me to pound sand. The man didn't build a sports-entertainment empire from the ground up by pondering the suggestions of others. He runs purely on his instincts. The only thing he's thinking about is the best way to punish me.

Charlie turns his attention to Lucy, going over the plan for an upcoming match between two other wrestlers. Something about a human joining the roster. This should pique my interest, but I'm too busy trying not to freak out to care. I attempt to ignore their conversation by doing jump squats.

By the time Charlie finally leaves the gym, I'm drenched in sweat. Lucy shoots me a confused look with all three heads, brows creased.

"Why did you work yourself so much already?" Her left head asks. "We were going to work on your acrobatics today, but I don't know if we can now that you've done all those jump squats."

I frown. "I needed the distraction."

Her middle head rolls its eyes. "You're impossible. Go work on upper body until your meeting with the head writer. Goddess knows you've done enough lower body already."

Perfect. My favorite ways to blow off steam are bench presses and biceps curls. Nothing makes me feel stronger. It will also give me time to think about what I should prepare for dinner tonight with Iris. It's my turn to host, and I want to blow her takeout sushi out of the water.

After a cathartic gym session and a fun meeting with the head writer, where we discussed my upcoming live promo with Iris to promote our MonsterMadness match, I head to the locally sourced market across the street from my condo. This shop was a big reason I even bought the place. I love to cook, and I wanted quick and easy access to the best ingredients within walking distance.

I fill my basket with all the items needed to make creamy mushroom pasta with homemade noodles, a side salad, and fresh crusty bread. And since Iris loves dessert so much, I grab the ingredients for a lemon ricotta cake. Might as well knock her socks off. Maybe it'll be so good that she'll drop to her knees and apologize for being such a bitch to me all the time.

Ha! Fat chance. But it's worth a try.

When I get home, I put on a classical music record and immediately get to work. While I'm an excellent cook, I'm also slow and methodical with my technique. Cooking is a passion of mine, and I like to savor the art of it. There's no rushing in my kitchen.

Just as I'm dropping the fresh-cut noodles into boiling water, there's a knock on my door. Perfect timing. I'll have just enough time to get her settled right before the pasta reaches al dente.

Chapter 8

Iris

I SCOWL AS I RIDE the elevator. Of course, Lena lives in a penthouse suite. She probably judged my cozy little studio. I could afford something larger and more extravagant if I wanted to, but I can't bring myself to spend money when I'm perfectly happy with what I have.

When the elevator opens to reveal a massive open floor plan decked out in modern blues and grays, I can't say I'm surprised. But what does shock me is that it's not cold and uninviting. In fact, it's quite swanky and welcoming. She must have hired an interior designer. The only thing off-putting is the distinct lack of art on the walls. The space could really use some fun pops of color.

The scowl melts from my face when I smell cooking butter, cream, and garlic. My mouth starts watering at the heavenly aroma. I didn't realize I was that hungry.

"Welcome to my humble abode, Iris," Lena says with a smirk. She's wearing a casual green T-shirt dress and a black apron that reads *Kiss The Chef*. Dangling from her horns are two strands of golden beads, complementing her gold necklace. I'm severely underdressed in my matching purple athletic set of shorts and a strappy tank top.

She continues, "Make yourself at home. But first, what would you like to drink? I have water, all temperatures and fresh-squeezed lemonade."

"I'll take lemonade, thanks."

I fight back the urge to snap at her. It's just like Lena to rub in my face the fact I didn't have her precious room-temperature water available when she came over for dinner. And to have fresh-squeezed lemonade? What a show-off.

"Here you go." Lena hands me a cold glass of lemonade garnished with a plump strawberry.

"Fuck," I murmur after taking a sip. That's fresh. And it has the perfect balance of sweet and tart. I was hoping it would suck.

"What's wrong?" she asks as she drains a pot of boiling water.

"Nothing. Your lemonade is really good."

Lena laughs. "Did I just get a compliment from you?"

I glare at her over the top of my glass as I take another sip. As much as I hate myself for it, I can't stop drinking the tasty beverage.

She shakes her head, the beads hanging from her horns clicking as she adds the drained pasta to the simmering sauce on the stove.

"Did you cook?" I ask, setting my lemonade on the island to avoid gulping the rest of it down.

"Yes." Lena nods. "Cooking is one of my passions."

"Oh."

I didn't know this about Lena. Honestly, it surprises me a little that she doesn't have a private chef. She always struck me as too privileged to do anything as mundane as cooking her own meals. I guess you can't judge someone without getting to know them.

And now that I think about it, I don't know much about Lena of the Minotaur Clan, other than that she's a pain in the ass. But isn't that the point of this entire thing? To "bond" with her?

Lena plates our meal, refills my lemonade, then starts a new record with ease. I'm surprised yet again. Who knew Helen Stronghorn, the reigning EMW Champion, was so domestic? She's not as much of a prissy princess as I thought. It almost makes me respect her.

My mouth starts to water when she slides my plate across the counter. *Fuck.* It looks and smells delectable. I fork a generous bite and shovel it into my mouth as gracefully as I can, hoping Lena doesn't notice how desperate I am to eat her cooking.

The moan that slips from my mouth is borderline obscene. The mushrooms have a pleasant firmness, while the sauce packs a mouth-watering savory and buttery taste. As for the pasta, I don't think I've ever had a more perfectly cooked noodle.

Lena quirks an eyebrow. "Good?"

I nod. "Incredible."

"Thank you," she responds with a dazzling smile.

Her grin drops when the phone rings. She rises from her seat and clacks over to the wall where the receiver hangs, cringing when she reads the caller ID.

"I have to answer this," she explains, her shoulders drooping and curving in as if she's trying to make herself smaller.

I nod. Not that she needs my approval or anything.

"Hello?" Lena answers as she walks down the hall. The sound of a door closing softly behind her indicates that she doesn't want me to overhear whatever conversation she's having.

Do I keep eating my pasta? It feels wrong to eat without her. I may not like Lena at all, but there's no point in going out of my way to be rude when she has been such a gracious hostess so far.

So I close my eyes and savor the melodic sound of the music, surprised once again. Who would have thought Lena had such great taste, let alone that she would care enough about sound quality to play a record?

I'm interrupted a few minutes later by a deep sigh as Lena comes back into the kitchen area, ears flat against her head. "Sorry about that."

"No problem."

She looks dejected, her shoulders slumped and her eyes downcast. Gone is the confident Lena who naturally owns both the ring and the kitchen. Who called, and what did they say? I've never seen her like this. It's unsettling.

"You waited for me?" She looks at my plate.

"Well, yeah. I didn't want to be rude." I shift in my seat.

I brace myself for a quip about how I'm always rude, or something along those lines. Instead, Lena just murmurs her gratitude before taking an unenthusiastic bite of pasta. This is weird. If there's one thing I know about Lena, it's that she never misses an opportunity to rag on me.

"Um…are you okay?" The question is out before I think it all the way through. As if Lena would ever share with her whatever happened.

"My dad called."

I startle. "The Mighty Minos?"

Lena grunts. "That was Victor, yes."

It takes me a moment to realize she is telling me her father's real name. I have never heard it before. Even among people in the industry, he's referred to as "The Mighty Minos" or just Minos for short.

My heart starts to race. Is her father alright? Something horrible must have happened for her to be acting like this.

I start to stand. "What happened? Do we need to reschedule dinner so you can go help him?"

She rolls her eyes. "Hardly.

I cock my head, confused about her callous response as I settle back into my seat. "But…then why are you so…bummed now?"

"It may come as a shock to you, but Victor can be a bit of an asshole."

I cough. Did she just call her dad an 'asshole?' "Wait. Can you repeat that?"

She stabs a mushroom with her fork with a little too much force, causing a loud clanking sound that makes me clench my teeth.

"I called him an 'asshole,' Iris."

"Did you…do something?"

I can't imagine The Mighty Minos being anything other than a kind monster. He was my *hero,* for goddess's sake.

The instant the question leaves my mouth, I instantly regret it. Lena's face darkens as she slams her fork on the counter.

"You just don't get it, do you?"

The venom in her voice is unlike anything I've heard before. Most of the time, her comments are filled with impatient disapproval, but this time, her response is filled with a desperate loathing. It's like she's begging me to understand why she hates me.

Instead of getting pissed off, my heart breaks a little. There's something about seeing someone's spirit crushed that resonates with me, especially someone as fiery as Lena—even if I hope her pillow is too hot on both sides.

"Help me understand," I plead softly, leaning closer to her.

Lena's eyes search mine. I give her a small smile, hoping to communicate that my request is genuine.

Finally, her shoulders and ears relax. "Being the daughter of arguably the greatest wrestler of all time isn't all it's cracked up to be."

My brows pinch. "How is that? You had all the advantages most of us wish we had!"

Lena scoffs. "But it came with a price! Tell me. What did you do during the summer as a kid?"

"I usually played outside with the neighbor kids." I shrug. "We even managed to save up enough to go to the beach a few times."

"Sounds fun. I never got to do anything like that."

"Go to the beach?"

She shakes her head. "I never got to play."

I cover my mouth with my hand. "What? Why not?"

"As soon as I expressed interest in being a wrestler like my dad, he threw me into training and wrestling camps." Lena pushes the pasta around on her plate with her fork while glaring at it. "It sounds like a great opportunity, and it was, but it also sucked. While all the other kids in school came back from summer break talking about all the fun adventures they'd gone on, I didn't have anything to share because I couldn't even tell anyone! Charlie doesn't like the curtain to be pulled back on our industry, as you know, so what I did over the summers was a secret."

"Oh." I'm honestly too stunned to say much more.

"Yeah." The words come pouring out of her like a dam has broken inside her. "And as if that weren't bad enough, my dad expects a lot from me. I have a 'legacy' to uphold. Do you know what that means? That means I must be *perfect* all the damn time. I can't fuck up. Mistakes aren't an option for me."

Lena pauses to catch her breath before diving back into her diatribe. "And you know why my dad called me just now? To tell me how disappointed he was in me for expressing that I didn't want to waste my time doing this dumb dinner with you. I doubt we're ever going to get along, so what's the point?"

I open my mouth to offer some semblance of comfort but immediately snap it closed. Lena is upset, and I doubt there's anything I, her least favorite person in the realms, can say that will cheer her up.

"Good." She narrows her eyes. "Keep your shitty comments to yourself."

"I wasn't going to say anything shitty!"

"Oh yeah? What were you going to say, then?"

I look down at my plate. Do I tell her that I wanted to console her? She probably wouldn't believe me anyway. But I need to show Lena that I'm not a total bitch. Lena just opened up to me. How do I show her that I respect that?

"My mom once had to put out a fire when I tried to cook rice," I blurt out.

Goddess. Why is this the first story that popped into my head? Maybe it's my way of telling Lena that I appreciate her cooking. Or maybe it's my way of also opening up, too, in a way that will lighten the mood.

Lena snorts. "What?"

"I was seven, and I was really craving fried rice. Instead of asking my mom how to do it, I tossed dry, uncooked rice in a hot pan and then promptly forgot about it when I got distracted by the book I was reading. I'd didn't remember until my mom came running into the kitchen screaming about something burning."

"I bet your mom was pissed." She cackles

"I'm sure she was. I would have never known, though. She was always so patient with me. She even taught me how to make fried rice as soon as we were done cleaning up my mess."

"Your mom sounds like a wonderful female," Lena remarks, her expression soft.

"She is," I agree with a happy sigh. "I couldn't have asked for a better mother."

Lena grins at me. We gaze at each other, smiling like goofs for a few moments before she clears her throat. "I guess we should finish eating before it gets too cold."

"Oh." I load another forkful. "Even cold, I bet it would still be delicious."

"Honestly, you're probably right," she says, tossing her hair over her shoulder.

There's the confident Lena I know.

"Don't let it get to your head." I hide my smile behind a mouthful of crusty bread, pleased my little story worked as intended. Lena is in a much better mood now.

Her tail flicks in annoyance. "What's that saying? 'Don't bite the hand that feeds?'"

"Maybe that hand needs a nibble or two before it gets too cocky," I say, eyeing her.

Lena may be frowning at me, but her eyes sparkle with mirth. "Don't nibble too much. You gotta save room for dessert."

I perk up. "You made dessert, too?"

"Yes!" She laughs. "A lemon ricotta cake."

"I've never even heard of that, but it sounds tasty!"

"I'm not as good of a baker as I am a cook, but I'm sure it will still be fine," she says with a shrug.

"Is that modesty I'm hearing?" I tease, holding a hand to the shell of my ear.

She crosses her arms over her chest. "Shut up, Iris! Eat your dinner before I regret being so nice to you."

"Is this what you call nice?" I ask with a snicker.

Lena gasps. "I made a whole cake! That's very thoughtful of me."

"Fine." I put my hands on my hips. "I'll agree. But only if you let me take home the leftover cake."

"Deal."

A free cake? Maybe Lena isn't too bad after all.

Chapter 9

Lena

"MOTHER! MOTHER! MOTHER!" CHEERS THE crowd, waving countless signs of support for me.

I smile and wait for them to quiet down. The showrunners allotted time for crowd chanting, especially since I'm a fan favorite, but I still have to keep them on track, so when the cheering doesn't seem to be stopping, I hold up a finger, asking for silence.

And being the amazing fans that they are, they cease their cheers. It's good being a babyface.

"Thank you for the warm welcome, Metro Bay!" I coo into the microphone.

The crowd goes nuts again, but as soon as I open my mouth, they quiet down.

"As we approach MonsterMadness, I'm at a loss. Do you know why?" I pout, jutting out my lip further than usual to play to the cameras.

"Why?" the audience asks in unison.

"Because no one has stepped up to challenge me for the Realms Championship. I asked Mr. Palmer who would be challenging me at the main event, and he told me no one is up for it. He said, and I quote, 'Everyone is too scared of you.' So I guess the championship remains with me. This means that, unfortunately, you won't get a MonsterMadness Main Event match from— "

As I expected, but to the surprise of the audience, the heavy metal music of Athena Rainstorm interrupts my speech. The crowd immediately erupts into a chorus of jeers, possibly even louder than the welcome they gave me. Some hate Athena more than they love Helen.

I roll my eyes, shooting the camera pointed at me a conspiratorial scoff. Outside, I radiate annoyance that Athena is interrupting my time to shine, but on the inside? I'm a little nervous. This is the first promo Iris and I have ever done together. Will we have good chemistry? Will our actual hatred for each other poison the promo?

But after last night, I'm starting to wonder if we could learn to at least tolerate one another. We briefly spoke before I came out to the ring, making sure we agreed on the high points of our promo, and to my surprise, we were civil. I guess the other night's dinner really was a bonding experience.

Iris smirks as she slips through the ropes, mic in hand. "You thought you were going to get off easy, didn't you, Helen Stronghorn?"

The audience's boos are thunderous. While Iris maintains her cocky grin, something akin to hurt flashes in her eyes. That's odd. What was that wounded look? I file the question away for future Lena to mull over.

"What do you want, Miss Rainstorm?" I growl.

"What everyone wants, whether they are willing to admit it or not."

I cock my head. "And what would that be?"

"I have a challenger for you for MonsterMadness."

The collective mix of gasps, boos, and cheers forces me to pause before I ask the obvious question. "And who would that be?"

The arena is so quiet, you could hear a pin drop.

"Me!" Iris spreads her wings wide.

The crowd erupts, their screams so loud they hurt my ears. I knew a match between Athena Rainstorm and Helen Stronghorn would be well-received, but not like *this.* I should have brought earplugs. Iris's eyes widen a fraction. I'm pretty sure she's also surprised.

We let the audience have their moment. They've been waiting for this matchup. Besides, Iris and I can't speak until they calm down. To add to my character's disdain, I scan her, as if sizing her up.

I haven't taken a long look at Iris since we first met. And damn, she's still as gorgeous as ever. From her stunning eyes, all the way down to her dangerous talons. My gaze lingers a little too long on her hips and breasts. How would they feel under my grip? What color are her pert nipples straining against her spandex leotard?

Oh fuck. No. I was *not* just thinking about Iris of the Harpy Clan's nipples.

My cheeks burn. Thank all the goddesses in all the realms that I'm covered in fur. If Iris notices me creeping on her body, she doesn't let on, instead continuing to glare at me. It's a good thing she's such a professional.

By the time the audience settles, I've also calmed enough to deliver the next line. "You think you're gonna just waltz into MonsterMadness and take the title from me?"

Iris peers at an imaginary speck of dirt under her nails. "Like it's hard?"

"You better look at me when I'm talking to you."

Iris narrows her eyes at me. "Nah. I'm tired of looking at your smug, ugly face."

The audience boos. It's a cheap way to generate heat but an effective one.

"You better get used to it, Miss Rainstorm, because this"—I wave my hand in front of my face—"isn't going anywhere."

"So, you admit it? You agree you're ugly?"

We had discussed that Iris was going to call me ugly, but we both prefer improv for our live promos. It was a stupid decision. Not because I'm actually offended—I'm gorgeous—but because the line is so just so damn good that I have to bite my bottom lip to keep me from smiling. Here's to hoping I still look menacing.

She sneers. "Don't worry, though. Maybe your face just needs a little rearranging via my fist."

The crowd goes nuts. Iris is a master on the mic. She may be a heel, but the audience is putty in her hands, playing into every snide remark.

I step closer to Iris until we are less than a foot apart. "You're either blind or have horrible taste. I'm gorgeous. Ask anyone. Better get your eyesight checked before our match."

The audience cheers at my comeback, and Iris claps along before suddenly cocking back her hand and springing herself into the air to slap me across the cheek. I stumble back, exaggerating the impact of her hand across my face.

I play up checking to see if I'm bleeding. Of course, I'm not, but the fans don't know that. Iris's laugh is maniacal, sounding like an evil villain from a human superhero movie. The crowd is on their feet, shouting for me to retaliate.

With a determined scowl, I charge at Iris, horns first. But at the last moment, she flaps her wings and takes to the air. I crash into the ropes.

"I'll see you at MonsterMadness...bitch," she snarls before dropping the mic between my horns and flying out of the arena.

I take my time dragging myself out of the ring toward the backstage, passing by my supportive, yet outraged fans. They reach their hands over the barricades, desperate for acknowledgment. I make sure to slap as many hands as I can. Not only is this expected of me as a babyface, but I adore the enthusiasm they have for me.

When I finally stumble into the staging area and out of public view, I allow myself to laugh. That live promo was incredible! I usually watch my promos after they've aired to get an idea of how I can improve, but I have a feeling I'll have no notes on this one. Thank the goddess because I sometimes I just want to relax afterward. But my legacy demands perfection, and I can't be perfect unless I'm constantly improving.

"Lena?" A production assistant grabs my attention. "Mr. Palmer wants to see you and Iris in his office. Now."

Well, that's killed my glee real fast. That promo was perfect! What more could he have wanted from us? I look around for Iris, hoping to aim my indignation at her, but I don't see her. She must have already been summoned. If this went bad in Charlie's eyes, it's her fault, not mine.

I sigh. But that's not fair. Nor is it true. Iris rocked that promo. But so did I. What is there to improve on?

This question rattles around in my head as I clop my way to wherever Charlie's office has been set up. Zach nods at me as I approach, letting me know I can enter. I open the door. Iris is sitting rigidly in front of Charlie. He leans all the way back in his chair, feet on the desk.

"Lena! My girl! Come in!" He waves me toward the empty chair next to Iris. "I just wanted to discuss tonight's promo."

I lower myself into the chair next to Iris, sparing her a side glance. Her features are perfectly neutral, but I've come to know her better than that. The small quiver in her hands indicate that she's as scared shitless as I am.

"I think you two owe me some gratitude," Charlie says with a pompous grin.

"Sir?" Iris returns.

"How many times do I gotta tell you to drop the 'sir?'"

"My apologies, s—I mean, Charles."

"That's better. What was I saying? Oh yeah. You two should be thanking me."

Iris and I stare at our human boss, not responding. What the fuck is he talking about?

Charlie sighs. "For making you two spend time together outside of training. The chemistry between you two is off the charts! And we would have never gotten that if you continued to be at each other's throats."

"Umm…" I'm still confused. "I don't mean to assume for Iris, but I don't think we're exactly friends or anything."

"And that's fine!" Charlie laughs. "As long as you two can get along well enough to work together, I'm happy. And, boy, am I happy. Did you hear that crowd? They *love* your rivalry!"

Iris and I exchange side glances. Charlie didn't call us in here to scold us? Is he actually pleased? But neither of us react just yet.

"Oh, come on!" Charlie leans forward. "Why the long faces?"

"And what does that mean for us?" Iris asks, surprising me by speaking up.

"It means more promos, more TV time, and, more importantly, keeping up what you're doing. I don't want you two to slip back into old habits. Have you even started planning your match yet?"

My face flushes. *Shit.* We haven't planned anything beyond the suplex off the top rope, and we didn't even come up with that ourselves.

Neither of us says a word. The silence is deafening.

Charlie frowns. "Not even the big finisher?"

When we don't answer, he lets out a long sigh. "Listen. You two are my main event. We *can't* fuck this up. I expect the best match I've ever seen from Helen Stronghorn and Athena Rainstorm. Do you understand?"

"Yes, sir," Iris agrees.

At the same time, I say, "Of course, Charlie."

His gaze darts between the two of us. After a few moments, he sits back in his chair. "Good. Before the show next week, I expect you two to have figured out the big finisher." Charlie waves us off. "You may leave now."

Iris rises from her seat. "Thank you" She wastes no time scurrying out of his office.

I continue to sit, brows furrowed. Spending that extra time with Iris probably *did* help our in-ring chemistry, but that doesn't mean I want to keep wasting my precious free time hanging out with her.

"You have something to say, Lena?" Charlie cocks his head. "How's your father doing? Have you talked to him recently?"

This isn't a genuine question. No, this is a threat. He'll get my dad involved if he has to.

I swallow. "Yes. Just the other night," I answer.

"Well, if you talk to him again before I do, tell him I send my love."

"Of course." I stand.

"Great talk, Lena," Charlie says with a small wave.

I force a smile and turn around, eager to get the hell out of his office. Once I close the door behind me, I let out the breath I've been holding.

"You okay?"

I startle at Iris's voice, letting out a small yelp. Ugh. That was not very tough bitch of me.

"Oops. Sorry. Didn't mean to scare you."

"You didn't—" I start to argue but stop myself. Maybe not right outside Charlie's office. "Never mind. Yeah. I'm fine. Just ready to go back to my hotel and get some rest."

Iris's expression softens. "Same. Normally, I like to go out after a show, but I'm just not feeling it tonight."

Together, we head toward the locker room.

"Our promo was kind of fun, wasn't it?" I ask with a sheepish grin.

She smiles. "Yeah. Not bad for our first promo. I hate to admit it, but I'm kind of looking forward to our next one."

"Me, too." I glance at her, admiring the way her eyes sparkle.

Then I remember the flash of sadness in them during our promo.

"Hey," I begin, "do you like doing promos?"

Iris cocks her head. "What do you mean?"

I shrug. "I thought you looked a little sad out there."

"Oh." She stiffens. "Yeah. I mean, sometimes the audience gets t…"

"What? What is it?"

"Nothing." She shakes her head, as if erasing the thought from her mind. "I appreciate you checking on me, though."

I want to push to the issue but decide against it. We continue the trek to the locker room in comfortable silence. Is this what getting along with Iris feels like? We don't have to be best friends; we just don't have to be at each other's throats constantly.

When we reach the locker room, Iris rocks onto her back talons. "Well, I'm gonna grab my stuff. I guess I'll call you tomorrow with plans for our next 'mandated fun time.'"

I laugh. "Sounds good."

Maybe, just maybe, we can make this work.

Commercial Break

Big Foot Burrito

"UGH! LIL! I'M SO HUNGRY!" Fauna Piper groans, clutching her stomach.

She sits in the passenger seat of a two-door convertible with Lil Nightheart at the wheel.

"I have some carrot sticks in the back seat," Lil offers.

Fauna sticks out her tongue. "Yuck! I need something bursting with flavor."

Lil points to an upcoming convenience store. "What about some chips and candy?"

"I need something more filling."

"Burgers?"

"Ugh! No, thank you."

"Then what do you want?" Lil asks, rolling their black eyes.

Fauna gazes off into the distance. "I need something unique, something different, something…revolutionary."

Lil snaps their fingers. "I know!"

"You do?" Fauna perks up.

Lil takes a hard right, sending Fauna slamming against the side of the car.

"What are you doing?" Fauna screeches.

The scene cuts to Lil pulling the convertible into the parking lot with a large sign in green neon.

"Big Foot Burrito?" Fauna asks with an arched eyebrow.

"I know exactly what you need." Lil waves for Fauna to follow them inside.

A female sasquatch dressed in a bright-green uniform greets the two pro wrestlers with a large smile. "Hi! Welcome to Big Foot Burrito. What can I get for you?"

"Two Cryptid Burritos, please." Lil hands the cashier a wad of cash. "With extra Yeti Chill Ranch sauce."

Fauna cocks her head, her braids falling over her shoulder. "What's a Cryptid Burrito?"

A close-up shot of a large burrito fills the screen.

"A Cryptid Burrito is a warm, soft, foot-long tortilla *stuffed* with beans, rice, three kinds of cheese, guacamole, and smothered in Big Foot Burrito's zingy new Yeti Chill Ranch sauce," Lil explains in a voice-over.

The cashier sets a tray with two massive burritos between Lil and Fauna, who are now sitting at a booth.

"Whoa!" Fauna licks her lips. "You weren't kidding. These are really an entire foot long."

"You think that's impressive. Wait until you taste it," Lil encourages.

Fauna and Lil both take a massive bite of their burritos at the same time. A soft haze with sparkles surrounds the two while inspirational music swells.

"This is the best burrito I've ever had!" Fauna says around a mouthful of food.

"Is this what you were looking for?" Lil asks with a smile.

"Yes! Thank you, Lil, for taking me to Big Foot Burrito."

Lil turns, looking directly at the camera. "Big Foot Burrito…yes, it's *really* that big."

Chapter 10

Iris

I SCRIBBLE DOWN IDEAS ON the back of a piece of junk mail for Big Foot Burrito.

"Manicures?" I strike a line through the word. "Nah. Baking? Eh. Maybe." I doodle question marks next to the idea.

The memory of Lena admitting she didn't have a childhood replays in my mind. That's so sad. Don't get me wrong, there's still a part of myself that burns with jealousy at her privilege, but I don't envy that part of her upbringing.

What was one of my favorite things to do as a kid?

Oh! Craft time!

I loved sitting down with a pile of art supplies and creating something from my imagination. It was even better when I got to do it with my parents or friends. Maybe Lena would like that? I could order pizza and junk food, just like the slumber parties when I was a kid!

Time to call Lena. I skip to the phone, punch in her number, and bounce on my feet while I wait for her to answer.

"Hello?" she answers on the fifth ring. Not that I was counting or anything.

"Lena!" I wince at the excitement in my voice. *Way to play it cool.*

"Yes?"

"When are you free for our next 'mandated fun time?'" I ask, breathless. This is the greatest idea I've ever had. I'm practically a genius.

"Hold on," she responds. Her end of the line is silent other than the sound of shuffling papers. "I'm free tomorrow."

"Perfect!" I can't help the large grin that spreads across my face.

"Why do you sound so happy?" Lena's tone is wary.

"I have the best idea."

"What is it?"

"It's a surprise." I snicker. "Can you come over tomorrow afternoon? Around four o'clock?"

"You better not have something stupid planned," she growls.

What the fuck? I clench my fists. I'm trying to surprise her and this is how she responds? Maybe I shouldn't waste my time planning something special for Lena.

I attempt to control my temper. "Do you want to follow Charlie's orders or not?" Okay. I could have done better, but she really pisses me off sometimes.

A sigh. "Yes. Fine. Sorry. I'll be there at four."

"Thank you," I say with a sniff. "And wear comfy clothes that you don't mind getting dirty."

"Alright."

"Good."

A long silence.

"Are we done?" Her tone is clipped.

"Oh. Yeah. Umm…bye." I smash the disconnect button. Why am I so damn awkward?

Oh well. I can't dwell on it.

Time to start planning.

I observe my setup, hands on my hips, proud of what I've managed to pull together.

Pan and Daphne were sweet and accompanied me on my shopping excursion, so I didn't overthink everything. Painting had always been my favorite craft activity growing up, so I purchased two canvases and a variety of oil paints. After we left the hobby store, we hopped over to the market and filled an entire shopping cart with chips, sodas, and cookies from the bakery.

"You sure are putting a lot of effort into this date," Daphne said as we strolled through the candy aisle.

I rolled my eyes "It's not a date! Lena and I call it 'mandated fun time.'"

Pan stares at me. "You even have inside jokes?"

"It's not an inside joke," I responded, plucking a package of Twizzlers from the shelf, my favorite human candy.

"Sure. Whatever you say." Daphne handed me a package of Red Vines. "Here."

"Uh…Red Vines are gross."

"If there's one thing I know about you and Lena, it's that you two can't agree on anything." Daphne tossed the candy into the cart. "Take the Red Vines."

I shake my head, trying to forget the conversation with my friends. Why did it make me so uncomfortable? Whatever. Lena should be arriving in a few minutes.

Am I forgetting anything?

Chips and candy in bowls for easy access? Check. Canvases on easels? Check. Water cups for rinsing brushes? Check.

Oh! Music!

I rush to my CD tower. What makes me think of the slumber parties of my childhood? *I know! Boy bands!*

Snagging the entire discography of The Backstreet Boys, I load them into my multidisc CD player. The dulcet tones of Brian seep from my speaker system. *Perfect!*

A sharp knock on my door causes my smile to falter. Lena is here! *Oh shit!* What if she hates this idea?

Wait a second. Why do I care so damn much?

Another knock.

No time to think about *that.*

I answer the door. Lena stands in the hall, dressed in baggy sweatpants and a tank top that clings to her muscular curves.

Stop eyeing her body! Don't be a creep.

"Come in!" I step aside, giving Lena space to enter my apartment.

"Oh, wow!" Her eyes dart around the room, taking in my meticulous setup. "What is all of this?"

Crap. She wants an explanation, and now I feel awkward trying to explain. "Umm..." I fidget, my wings quivering. "I just thought maybe we could eat junk food and paint. Kind of like a slumber party. I was even going to order pizza."

Lena's jaw drops. "Slumber party?"

I nod. "But without the sleeping over part. You mentioned you didn't get to do fun stuff as a kid. I thought maybe you might enjoy a classic childhood experience. I understand if you think it's dumb, but—"

"I love it," Lena cuts me off, her words coming out in a sharp breath. She turns to me. "Seriously, Iris. This might be one of the nicest things anyone has ever done for me."

"Really?"

She smiles. "Yes."

I straighten my posture, wings held back and proud. "Great! Do you want to grab some snacks and get started?"

Lena grabs a plate off the counter. "Oh wow! Look at all the junk food." She picks up a Red Vine. "Awh! You got Red Vines?"

"Yeah." I brace myself, ready for a fight.

"They are my favorite." she says, taking a bite.

I stick out my tongue. "Twizzlers are superior."

"Your taste buds are fucked," she says with a laugh.

"Red Vines don't taste good dipped in nacho cheese. Therefore, Twizzlers are better."

Lena blinks at me. "You...dip your Twizzlers in nacho cheese?"

"It's delicious. Especially at the movies with some extra-buttery popcorn."

"Yep. My assessment stands."

I shrug. "Don't knock it till you try it."

She shakes her head, grinning, as she continues to pile her plate high. After pouring herself an icy cup of root beer, Lena picks a canvas, placing her snacks and drink on the craft table I borrowed from my neighbor with kids.

"What are we painting?" she asks, examining the various color options.

"Whatever you want," I say, standing in front of my matching blank canvas.

She rubs her chin. "I have no idea!"

I pick out paints in the primary colors. "I'm thinking something scenic."

"Oh!" Lena's ears perk. "That's a good idea."

"Just let me know when you start to get hungry for pizza," I say, picking out my brushes.

"Will do!" Lena's smile is bright.

Goddess. She's beautiful.

Umm...what the fuck, brain? Why on this goddess' green realm did I just think that? Looking away, I stare so hard at the blank canvas in front of me that I'm surprised I don't bore holes into it. I'm blaming the sappy music.

Lena and I start sketching on our canvases with pencils, singing along with the music. I draw a mountain scene, reminiscent of the Harpy Clan's ancestral home, while Lena outlines what appears to be a beach.

The experience of creating art next to Lena is a surprisingly pleasant one. We don't argue. There's no hostility. Just an occasional, "that looks great," or "I like the color you're using."

We order pizza when we start to get hungry, and by the time it arrives, we're ready for a break. After serving ourselves several slices of cheesy goodness, we sit on the stools around my kitchen island.

"Thank you," Lena says after swallowing her first bite of pizza.

"For what?"

"For doing this for me." She looks at me, tail swishing. "You hate me, but did something really nice for me."

My feathers ruffle. "I don't know. Maybe I don't *hate* you..."

Lena holds up a hand. "Wait. You *don't* hate me?"

I sigh, wings sagging. "I think at this point, I'm just bitter and jealous."

"Jealous?" Lena cocks her head.

Do I trust her to be this vulnerable? Lena shared a piece of herself with me at our last dinner. Not only does it seem fair to reciprocate, but it feels right.

"Yeah." I look down at my slice of pizza. "I didn't have a famous dad. My family didn't have much money growing up, so my parents couldn't afford to send me to wrestling camp or school, even though I begged and begged for it. With the little extra money we did have, we went on short family vacations. I have very fond memories of those vacations, don't get me wrong. But I wanted to be a wrestler so bad."

I glance at Lena. She's leaning forward as if my story is the most interesting thing she's ever heard.

"When we had career day at school," I continue, "I would spend hours crafting a championship belt from whatever I could, so I could go dressed as a pro wrestler. Everyone laughed at me. But I didn't care. It was my dream. Still is, if I'm being completely honest."

"But your dream came true. You're a pro wrestler now," Lena interjects.

"But I've never been a champion."

She averts her eyes. "Oh."

"So I had to work really hard. I scraped every piece of copper to afford wrestling school, then spent years on the independent circuit, proving myself. It's embarrassing, but I was honestly so excited to meet you. You're the daughter of my hero! How cool is that?"

Lena snorts but doesn't say anything, allowing me to continue.

"However, when I met you and you snubbed me, I was hurt. Was I not good enough? Then when I saw the way you treated others, as if you were the most important entertainer in the EMW? I couldn't stand you. So many of us worked our asses off for our opportunities while you just waltzed in as the ultimate babyface, compliments of The Mighty Minos? I just couldn't accept it."

I'm met with silence. Did I take it a step too far? No one enjoys hearing why someone thinks they suck.

"I…had no idea," Lena finally says. "Do…other people feel this way about me?"

I lean away, surprised she asked. "Uh…I can't speak for others."

She looks down, her brows creasing. "You can't be the only one, though. I just didn't know I gave that impression."

"Oh…umm…I mean, it's probably just me." I don't know why I have the urge to comfort my sworn rival right now.

"I knew I had an advantage being the daughter of The Mighty Minos, but I never thought about how it must feel for someone who didn't have that kind of help." Lena looks at me, her big brown eyes shining. "I'm sorry, Iris. I never meant to make you feel that way. Actually, if we're being honest with each other, I was a little intimidated by you when we first met."

"Intimidated?" I nearly choke on my pizza. "By me?"

"Yeah." She looks down at her hooves. "I was stunned to silence by how pretty you are."

A blush creeps up my cheeks. "You don't mean that," I say, rubbing the back of my neck.

"I do. And now I feel like such a bitch. Not only was I a jerk to you when we met, but I never thought once about my privilege."

As if propelled by someone who isn't me, I place a hand on top of Lena's. I've never touched her without being told to before. "It's okay. I mean, I know now that it's not that simple."

She looks at our hands, her mouth forming a thin line. I jerk my hand back. "Sorry," I murmur.

My hand feels cold without hers beneath mine.

"No," she says, her voice rising. "Uh…it's okay. I am just… You've never…" Lena clears her throat. "What do you mean it's 'not so simple?'"

"I mean I know now that you may have been training since you were a kid, but that meant a big sacrifice for you. You didn't get the childhood I had."

Lena gives me a half smile. "I didn't mean to make this about me."

"Well, my feelings have to do with you." I chortle.

Her smile reaches her eyes, and I once again find myself basking in her beauty.

"This pizza is really good," Lena says, taking another bite.

"It's my favorite! It's honestly one of the reasons I wanted a place in this neighborhood."

"You picked where to live based on the *pizza?*"

"You didn't?"

She laughs, and any remaining tension from our previous conversation dissipates.

After pizza, we get on the topic of childhood crushes.

"Oh, I just loved Barry," she coos, her tail swishing.

"You mean the one-hit wonder basilisk? But he was such a tool. There's a reason his music never got popular besides that one song."

"Tell that to my younger self." She giggles. "I didn't realize I only liked women yet, but looking back now, it's pretty obvious I liked him for his long hair and thick lashes."

I throw back my head and laugh. "His lashes aren't even that thick."

"Okay, Miss Judgmental." She waggles a paintbrush at me. "Whose name did you doodle in your notebook?"

"Every member of the Pegasus Ponies."

Lena sputters. "You have got to be kidding me? They were the most bubblegum of all the pop princesses."

"Yeah." I sniff. "And I still have all their CDs."

"But your entrance music is metal. I would've never guessed you were into such girly music."

I shrug. "My gay outweighs my musical preferences."

A roar of laughter erupts from her, echoing off the walls of my apartment. It's so infectious that I can't help but join in.

"Alright!" Lena declares once our laughter settles down. "I'm done!"

"I'm almost done, too!" I bite down on my lower lip, adding one last highlight to a flower in the valley I've painted.

Lena steps behind me and leans forward, close enough for me to catch the scent of her soap. Is that cinnamon and vanilla?

"That looks awesome!" she says. "Harpies live in such a beautiful place?"

"Most of us prefer the mountains, yes."

"I love the fluffiness of your clouds. They look good enough to eat."

I smile. They do look like tufts of cotton candy.

"Let's see yours." I move to stand in front of Lena's canvas. The painting takes my breath away. "Holy shit!"

A beautiful painting of a beach at sunset is displayed on the easel. The vibrant oranges and purples of the sky caught my attention first, but it's the way those colors reflect in the water that truly makes the piece amazing.

"Lena!" I breathe. "Wow! This is incredible. Do you know how beautiful this is?"

She frowns. "Is it?"

"How can you not tell?"

Lena shrugs. "I guess I've been looking at it too long."

"You have a hidden talent as a artist."

She sits up straight. "You mean that?"

"I do."

It's at that exact moment the current disc playing comes to a stop with a click.

Lena glances around, gaze landing on the digital clock above my stove. "Shit. It's *that* late?"

"Oh shit! Seriously? Fuck. We have to be at the gym early tomorrow, and I need my beauty sleep."

"I guess that means I should get going." She rubs her arm.

"Yeah. Probably for the best."

"Do you need help cleaning all this up?"

"Nah. I'll probably have this all this squared away by the time you get home."

"Are you sure?"

"I'm sure. Thank you, though. I appreciate it."

Lena reaches for her canvas, then pauses, frowning. "My painting is still wet."

"Oh. I can bring it to you once it's dry."

Her tail swishes. "Really? Are you sure?"

"Absolutely."

She smiles. "Great! Thank you, again."

I walk her to the door. "See you tomorrow?"

"See you tomorrow."

Chapter 11

Lena

"Ah! It feels good to be back at the old gym," my father says, sucking in a deep breath through his nose. "Smells like sweat and disinfectant. Just as it should."

I wrinkle my snout. Why did he have to mention the way it smells? Yuck.

"Why the weird face, daughter? Do you not love the scent of hard work?" He twitches his red ears. I received my coloring from my father, while my mother was a black-and-white minotaur.

"Um…that's not it," I reply. "I just didn't expect you to draw attention to it."

He laughs. "When you're old and retired, you'll miss smells like this. Now, where is Iris? I can't wait to meet her. I'm glad you made a friend in her, by the way."

"She's not—" I cut myself off. "She should be here any minute."

My instinct is to argue against any friendship between me and Iris. We've been at each other's throats for so long. But where do we stand now? After the painting party, the idea of hating her feels preposterous. How can I dislike someone who went out of her way to plan such a special surprise for me?

Which is why I'm at the gym extra early with my dad at my side. I want to return the kind and thoughtful favor. *Shit.* What if she thinks my surprise is stupid? Like an idiot, I didn't run this idea by anyone first. It probably would have been a good idea to ask June or Gianna.

I consider asking my dad to leave when Iris enters the gym. She's wearing a matching bright-pink athletic set today. It hugs every curve, the color making her gray skin look warm and touchable and oh, my goddess! Why am I thinking about touching the skin of Iris of the Harpy Clan? Get it together!

Her eyes become as round as the moon when her gaze lands on my father. "The Mi—"

"Please," my dad interrupts, stepping forward, hand extended, "call me Victor."

Iris takes his hand, clamping her mouth shut. "Wow. I…uh…I grew up watching you. You inspired me."

"And now you're a pretty darn good wrestler," he says with a smile.

Her mouth forms a perfect O. "You think…I'm…good?"

"Oh yeah! I've watched your matches. I'm honored and flattered an old bull like me could be such an inspiration to a skilled wrestler such as yourself."

It's at this moment that Iris's attention lands on me. They narrow, the movement probably unnoticed by anyone but me. Is she mad? I shift from one hoof to the other.

"Thank you, sir," she says, finally letting go of my dad's hand.

"Victor, please." He laughs. "Any friend of my daughter's is a friend of mine."

She cocks her head. "Friend?"

I clear my throat. "I figured Lucy could use a day off and thought it might be fun to have my dad train us today."

Her face breaks out in a gorgeous smile. "Me? Trained by The Mighty Minos?"

My dad pounds his chest with a fist. "That's right. And I won't go easy on you just because you're my daughter's friend. I never went easy on Lena."

Iris squares her shoulders and gives her wings a sharp snap. "Great, because I would hate if you treated me any differently. I'm more than capable."

My father turns to me. "I like her."

I gaze at Iris, admiring the way she holds herself with such determination and confidence. "Me, too," I murmur, quieter than a gentle breeze.

But her gaze flicks to mine for the briefest of moments. Did she hear me?

"Alright!" My dad claps his hands. "Let's see where you two are at with your suplex."

Iris and I demonstrate the suplex several times on the mat before my father asks us to move to the ring. When we climb to the top rope, she hesitates. She's nervous about hurting me, she explains. What if we don't get the angle of the landing right?

"I trust you, Iris. I know you'll do everything you can to protect my neck."

"But..."

"No 'buts.' If anyone has this, it's you."

She nods as she furrows her brow and squares her shoulders.

Drenched in sweat and near exhaustion, Iris and I decide to try one more time before calling it quits. We get into position on the top rope, chest-to-chest, with me facing the ring. Iris puts me in a choke hold, and I'm careful not to jab my horns into the base of her wings. Her free hand fists the waistband of my shorts while I place both of my hands around her hips. With a heave, we jump in tandem, Iris falling back while I soar through the air. We both land on our backs with a crash. *Success!*

My father nods his approval. "Iris, what do you do now that you've effectively incapacitated Lena?"

Iris smiles brighter than the sun. "I pin her."

"Excellent." He waves his hand toward me. "Let's see how you'll do it. This is a big move, so you really need to the sell the pin."

"Alright." Iris looks at me. "You ready?"

"Yeap! Go for it."

Iris crawls toward me, dragging herself across the mat. When she reaches me, she positions herself above me before grabbing my legs, spreading them, and pressing her hips against mine to effectively pin my shoulders to the mat. We lock gazes, and her lips quirk into a small smile.

I'm already flushed from our workout, but a new heat creeps to my lower belly and between my thighs. Iris has me pinned in a way that makes me feel exposed and open, like I'm about to be penetrated. This is the first time she's ever pinned me, and it's kind of hot. I swallow thickly, unnerved by my arousal at Iris putting me in this position. For a brief moment, I forgot about everything and everyone around me.

Her cheeks darken to an adorable blue gray before she clears her throat and rolls off of me. She turns to my father. "How was that?"

He gives her a thumbs-up. "Very dominating. The crowd is gonna love it. I consider this a success!"

"Hell yes!" She jumps to a stand, flapping her wings. "Approval from The Mighty Minos? I'll take it!"

My father grins, arms crossed. "And it looked *good*, too. The in-ring chemistry between you two is off the charts."

I heave myself off the mat. "Thanks, Dad!"

"No problem, sweetheart," he replies, his voice tender and warm.

"Why are we celebrating?" Charlie's voice startles me. How is that man always sneaking up behind us?

"The big boss!" My father hops out of the ring to give Charlie a high-five. "Your main event just rocked a suplex off the top rope."

"No shit?" Charlie looks between me and Iris. "Congratulations, ladies! I'm proud of you."

I grin. "Thanks, Charlie."

Iris nods. "Appreciate it."

Charlie turns to my dad. "Now that you're here, we should catch up in my office. I recently acquired a new whiskey from the human realm."

My dad's ears perk. "Human whiskey? Count me in."

"Dad?" I snicker. "It's not even noon."

"But it's five o'clock somewhere, right? Yeehaw! Let's go, Charlie."

My dad drapes an arm over Charlie's shoulders, and, together, the two saunter out of the gym. I turn to Iris, opening my mouth to praise her for how hard she worked today, but snap my jaw shut when I see the pure venom in her stare.

"Why did you do that?" she asks through clenched teeth.

I take a step back. "What do you mean?"

"Why did you bring your dad here?"

My ears flatten. "Do you mean to tell me you *didn't* like training with The Mighty Minos?"

She crosses her arms. "Victor was awesome, but I want to get one thing straight right now, Lena."

"Oh yeah?" I can't help the sarcasm creeping into my voice. "And what's that?"

What the fuck kind of reaction is this? She should be thanking me for asking my dad to come out of retirement to train us. How can she be so ungrateful?

Iris jabs a finger against my chest. "I am *not* a charity case."

Wait. "What?"

She glares. "You heard me."

"Yeah, I heard you just fine." My tail flicks. "But I don't understand. You think I asked my dad to come here because I feel sorry for you?"

"Why else would you ask him?"

I scoff. "You're serious? Iris, I asked my dad to train us today because I know how much he meant to you growing up."

She continues to stare at me.

"And after you surprised me the other night, I wanted to return the favor."

Her cheeks darken to a deep blue. "Oh."

I place a hand on her shoulder. "I know we haven't always gotten along, but not everything I do is a slight toward you."

She shakes her head, eyes closed now. "I'm sorry. It's not fair to you that I'm always in fight mode when it comes to you."

"I get it. It's hard not to fall back into old habits."

"I'm so embarrassed." She buries her face in her hands.

I give her shoulder a light squeeze. "It's okay. I'll forgive you if you're done being mad at me."

She chuckles. "Deal."

"I'm glad that's cleared up," I say, removing my hand from her shoulder.

But my palm feels oddly cold and empty now, as if my skin misses being against Iris's.

"Should we even attempt talking over the match?" she asks.

"We're in such a good spot right now. I don't know if we should risk it."

The corners of Iris's mouth curve upward. "Our relationship is so delicate."

"But it's gotten better, right?" I lean in, maybe a little too eager to hear her thoughts on us.

She nods, her eyes sparkling. "For sure."

I can't stop the grin from spreading on my face. "Maybe we can discuss the match tomorrow over some core training?"

She laughs deep from her belly, the sound sending a tingling heat from my ears to my hooves. "Nothing like planks to get the creative juices flowing."

"Exactly."

Iris wipes away tears of laughter. "I hate to admit it, but 'mandated fun time' really helped."

"I'm right there with you. Should we plan another?" I can't help but step closer to Iris, despite there being no reason to do so.

"You know?" She rubs her chin. "I think we're good for now. Maybe if we get into another spat, but let's leave it for now. I'm sure you're ready for some real free time with your friends."

My tail droops, but I force a smile. "Uh…yeah. That makes sense."

"We good?" Iris asks with a quirked brow.

"We're good." The lie feels like ash in my mouth.

"Alright!" She hops out of the ring, snatching her water bottle as she makes her way to the gym's exit. "See you tomorrow for creative core time."

I give her a half-hearted wave but keep my tone light. "Bye."

Why am I disappointed? I should be *happy* to get my evenings back, right? I miss Gianna and June. But, for some reason, I also already miss Iris.

"Stupid," I mutter.

I step out of the ring and make my way to the weights. Maybe some squats will help me work through these confusing thoughts and feelings. But I'm not alone. Daphne has also shown up.

"Hey, Lena!" She waves, racking her weights. "I've been waiting to talk to you."

"Oh yeah?" My ears twitch. "What's up?"

She laughs, sweeping her long braids behind her shoulders. "Don't tell me you've been so wrapped up in my girl Iris that you forgot we're wrestling this week?"

Shit! I totally did forget. Fauna Piper challenged Helen Stronghorn to a match to prove Fauna's worth as a wrestler. She's slated to lose, but we're supposed to give Daphne a good match, showcasing her athletic ability. She plays an excellent heel, but the fans have been saying she can't wrestle, which couldn't be further from the truth.

"Ha!" Daphne points at me. "You *did* forget."

I scrub my face with my hands. "I'm so sorry, Daphne."

She simpers. "It's okay. Iris is a smoke show. I don't blame you for being too distracted to remember."

"It's not like that!"

"You mean to tell me you don't think Iris is sexy?" Daphne asks with a knowing smirk.

"I—I mean—"

She waves me off. "I'm just joking."

I clear my throat, hating how flustered Daphne's teasing is making me.

"Here." Daphne points to the rack of weight plates. "Let's chat about the match while we work out. Sound good?"

I nod. "I'm doing squats."

"Sounds good. We can take turns spotting."

By the time we're done working out the specifics of our match, my legs are burning. The good news is that Daphne and I have wrestled a few times in the past year in tag team matches, so we already know how the other works in the ring. One run-through the day before the show should suffice.

"Great!" Daphne says, panting from her last set of squats. "Thanks for working that out with me."

"No problem." I towel off the sweat from my forehead.

"Now you can go back to your regularly scheduled program of thinking too much about Iris."

I cough. "Excuse me?"

She winks.

"Don't wink at me!"

"Whatever you say." Daphne snickers. "If you'll excuse me, I have a meeting with the writers to figure out where my storyline goes after you kick my ass."

"But—"

"Don't worry, Lena. I'll keep your secret." She saunters toward the exit, her hooves clacking on the tile floor.

I groan, but I keep my mouth shut. It's best not to give Daphne more ammunition to tease me.

Well, shit. That didn't help those weird thoughts about Iris at all. Stupid Daphne. I would have been fine if she hadn't brought her up again. And I'm a little insulted. Me? Think about the harpy too much? Give me a break. I barely think about her.

But that's not exactly true. Iris has been like a buzzing gnat ever since we met. Every interaction I have with her bugs me for days afterward. And it's even more complicated now that we're almost friends. I'm hanging onto her every word and actually *disappointed* she doesn't want to spend any more time together.

What is wrong with me?

I'm too tired to do any more exercises. Time to turn to my tried-and-true distraction—cooking. Maybe baking a metric fuck ton of quiches will take my mind off Iris.

But four hours later, after my fifth quiche and billionth time picturing Iris's brilliant smile and remembering the way she felt on top of me, I realize it's a lost cause. *Shit.*

Chapter 12

Iris

"Why am I like this?" I groan, collapsing onto my bed, wings spread to prevent crushing them.

Not only was I a total bitch to Lena about her bringing The Mighty Minos to train us, but I lied about thinking we didn't have to hang out anymore. I can't remember the last time I was this disappointed in myself.

Would being truthful have done me any good though? She didn't seem upset about getting her evenings back. And what about that weird moment between us when I pinned her? The fire that blazed through me at having Lena under me with her legs spread was searing and intense. There was a heat in her gaze, wasn't there? But what if I was wrong? I would have just embarrassed myself…again.

Even though I just fell into my bed, I already want to get back up again. Which doesn't make any sense. I should be exhausted after such a grueling training session. Why am I so restless?

Wait a second. When was the last time I had an orgasm? Shit. I can't remember, and that's really fucking sad. And maybe that would explain why I got so turned on when I pinned Lena.

Time to remedy the problem.

I reach into my nightstand and pull out my bright-blue vibrator with the sucking function. Let's hope it's still charged. I hold my breath as I press the power button and let it out when the toy hums to life.

I lift my sports bra, revealing my breasts. My nipples are already hard, aching to be touched. I slide my thumbs over the peaks as I try to envision the sexy scenes from my favorite romance novel.

It's easy. A human woman and a tall, beautiful, and buff orc. I like to put myself in the shoes of the human in this scene. The orc presses her smaller lover against a wall, spreading the human's legs with her knee. She slides her hands over the human's ass. I sigh and sink into the fantasy, imagining the orc woman gripping my hips. When my imaginary lover skates her hands up my stomach and over my breasts, my breath hitches in anticipation.

But instead of the orc's green hands, it's Lena's large red hands cupping my breasts that flashes through my mind.

No. Please no.

I close my eyes, trying again.

But this time, Lena is taking my nipple into her mouth, grazing it with her teeth.

Fuck. Okay. Maybe the spicy book isn't doing it for me.

I dig through my nightstand again, pulling out my stash of naughty magazines. Maybe some actual visuals will help.

In my favorite, I land on the centerfold, a succubus dressed as an angel in skimpy white lingerie and feather covers over her bat wings. I shimmy out of my pants, get on my knees, and hold the sucker function against my clit.

I jerk against the pulling vibrations. Fuck! That feels good. I stay focused on the succubus' glossy photo, desperate to fight the fantasy of Lena dipping her fingers inside me.

No luck. I toss the magazine off my bed with a frustrated groan.

Fuck it. I'll just think about Lena. Get it out of my system.

Closing my eyes, I fall back on my bed, pressing the toy harder into me. I imagine Lena's large body draped over mine, her hot breath on my neck as she rubs a thumb over my sensitive clit.

I reach between Lena's thighs, stroking her wet cunt. She groans over me, her red curls falling into her beautiful face. I bring my fingers to my mouth, tasting her.

When fantasy Lena slips her fingers into my pussy, I mirror the action on myself, gasping at how wet I am. But her fingers are larger than mine, so I add an extra digit, hoping to give myself the same sensation as if she were inside me. My hips buck. Goddess. I'm way too into this.

I ratchet up the strength of the suction as fantasy Lena whispers in my ear about how hot it is that I'm "wet and ready" for her. I nearly come when I picture her lowering her mouth between my legs, fingers still inside me, to circle my clit with her tongue.

When I imagine her thrusting her finger in and out of me while continuing to lick my clit, I turn up the intensity on my vibrator again. *Oh, goddess. I'm going to come.*

Fantasy Lena slides in another finger, and I add a third, spreading my fingers to give myself the stretch I imagine Lena would give me. *Fuck.* There's no stopping the freight train that is my orgasm.

"Lena!" I cry out, allowing ecstasy to wash over me.

My muscles tense, and my walls tighten around my fingers, soaking them. I arch my back, my wings spread wide as I finger fuck myself through my peak. When I finish, I let out a long sigh and melt into my bed.

That felt fan-fucking-tastic.

I lay in bed, panting and exhausted from my efforts. As my heart rate slows, it sinks inthat I masturbated to Lena of the Minotaur Clan. Did I really do that? A few weeks ago, I *hated* her, and now I'm thinking about her inside me. And the worst part is that I don't think I've ever come that fast before.

What am I going to do?

Chapter 13

Virginia Lavender

THE BELL RINGS THREE TIMES.

The crowd erupts in thunderous applause when a heavy guitar riff blares through the speakers. A moment later, Helen Stronghorn, dressed in her classic outfit—a sky-blue crop top, briefs, and chaps with silver trim—steps out from behind the LED screens displaying her branding. She flexes her biceps, and the audience explodes anew into cheers and whistles. The entrance music swells to its chorus, and I wince at how loud the stadium has become between the music and the fans.

"Please welcome to the ring—from the pastures of the Minotaur Clan—your EMW Champion, Helen Stronghorn!" Ivy shouts into the microphone.

As Helen saunters to the ring, she shakes the hands of children reaching over the barrier, offering them wide smiles and words of encouragement. Right before she climbs over the top rope, she looks around the arena and waves to her fans.

"Mommy knows best! Mommy knows best! Mommy knows best!" they chant in unison.

I nudge Nikolas with my elbow. "Hear that, Nik? They're cheering for their hero." This woman is wrestling royalty, and she always lives up to that legacy. She deserves this crowd's love.

"I do hear that." Nikolas rolls his eyes. "But who doesn't love Helen Stronghorn?"

Helen bounces from one hoof to the other, ready to start her match.

The music takes a more upbeat turn, like something heard at a house party, announcing the entrance of Fauna Piper. The satyr dances from behind the screens, wiggling her hips, her iridescent, long-sleeved crop top shining in the stadium lighting. Her long braids are looped into two buns on top of her head. I may be a Stronghorn fan, but there's something so fun about Piper.

The crowd is split. Half cheer, loving her carefree gimmick, while the other half boo, clearly not believing she has what it takes to challenge Stronghorn.

Ivy brings the microphone back to her mouth, a stoic furrow to her brow. "And her opponent, from the forests of Satyr Clan, 'The Dancer,' Fauna Piper!"

Fauna shimmies to the ring, ignoring the outstretched hands, but she does blow a few kisses to fans who are particularly enthused to see her. She smacks her haunches a few times before leaping into the ring.

"There's that sassy attitude we all know and love from The Dancer," Nikolas says.

"She's such a show-off." I roll my eyes despite enjoying the show Fauna is putting on.

The satyr does a cartwheel before landing in the splits with her hands in the air, beaming with confidence. Helen crosses her arms over her chest, tapping her hoof on the ring floor. With a graceful push, Fauna lands on her hooves, offering Helen a smirk.

The human official confirms with both wrestlers that they're ready before giving the signal. The bell rings three more times, indicating the start of the match.

"Let's see if Fauna can prove she deserves to be here at the EMW," I say, once again falling into my role of babyface enthusiast.

Nikolas snaps his beak. "You know she will. She's an incredible athlete, but she hasn't had the opportunity to show that off yet."

"Name the last time she won a match."

"That doesn't matter," Nikolas snaps. "What matters is that she can put up a good fight. Helen had better not underestimate Fauna."

Helen chops Fauna across the chest. Holding her hand over where she was struck, Fauna backs away until she reaches the ropes. She leans against them before springing forward and running toward Helen. The minotaur lowers her head, horns ready to collide with Fauna, but the satyr leaps, sailing over Helen's head and avoiding contact.

"Look at that show of athleticism!" Nikolas leans forward in his seat.

Fauna tucks and rolls before springing back up to her hooves, her brow furrowed. Growling, Helen charges again, and Fauna sidesteps, avoiding the champion.

I suck in a breath. "Nobody home! Helen isn't off to a great start here in this matchup."

With a roar, Helen charges for a third time, and, once again, Fauna avoids her. Fauna whirls around, wrapping her arms around Helen's waist. She grunts as she lifts Helen before slamming her opponent onto the mat.

Helen hisses, clutching her lower back. Fauna skips around the gasping champion, a smirk on her lips.

"This is awesome!" the crowd chants as they clap on beat.

Nikolas glances at me. "Now do you believe Fauna deserves to be here in the EMW?"

I nod. "She's proving herself tonight, I'll admit that."

Fauna continues to leap around Helen, waving her hands in the air and ignoring her opponent, so she lets out a sharp yelp when Helen snatches her ankle, jerking her to the mat. Fauna collides face-first with a loud smack, and Helen drags Fauna closer before positioning her into a Boston crab hold.

Many fans jump to their feet, eager to see if Fauna will submit. Fauna's face twists in pain, her teeth bared. The official drops to their knees, checking to see if she'll tap out.

Nikolas is suddenly on his feet. "Will Fauna give in?"

I'm awestruck. "I don't think so, Nik. She's fighting back."

In the ring, Fauna crawls toward the ropes while Helen struggles to keep her hold. The crowd cheers as Fauna reaches as far as she can, fingers grazing the bottom rope. With one final heave, she manages to grasp it. The official calls for Helen to let go.

"Damnit!" Helen drops Fauna's legs and whips around to glare down at her opponent. "Why don't you give up?" Helen's voice transmits over the stage mics to our headsets. "You'll never win against me."

Fauna's eyes narrow. "At least I'll go down trying!"

Using the rope, Fauna leaps, landing on her hooves before high kicking Helen in the face. Helen reels and crashes to the mat.

I jump from my seat, joining Nik, whose grip on our commentator table is turning his talon knuckles white. "Down goes the champ!" I shout through my gasp. "Can Fauna capitalize?"

Fauna is now limping over to Helen before collapsing to her knees. But she manages to lift Helen's legs and pin her shoulders.

"Oh, my goddess, Nik! The referee is down on their knees! They're going to start the count! Can you believe this?"

The human slams a hand against the mat.

"One!" the audience counts.

The official's hand comes down again.

"Two!"

Then, just as the official is about to connect with the ring floor again, it happens: Helen bucks her hips, sending Fauna tumbling off her.

Nikolas winces and seems to remember to sit back down. "And that's a kick out by Helen."

Both wrestlers lie on the mat now, gasping for air, seemingly exhausted. Helen crawls toward the ropes, clutching her snout, while Fauna rolls toward the apron. When Helen reaches the ropes, she pulls herself up. She looks around the ring, and when her gaze falls on Fauna, she bares her teeth.

Helen stalks toward Fauna, snatching one of her buns, and drags Fauna to a standing position. With a heave, she lifts Fauna above her head. She grins at the crowd, winks, and then drops Fauna, her knee colliding with Fauna's face.

"And Mother puts Fauna down for a nap!" I cheer, fluttering my wings, pleased to see Lena's finisher. She's still my favorite.

"It's over!" Nikolas shouts. "No way Fauna recovers from this."

Helen stares down at the limp body of Fauna. She shimmies her shoulders before dropping an elbow across Fauna's chest for good measure. Draping herself over the satyr, she waves for the official, who drops to their knees again and begin the count.

"One!"

All Fauna can do is groan.

"Two!"

Helen grins at the camera.

"Three!"

The bell rings three times.

"And your winner, by pinfall is…Helen Stronghorn!" Ivy drags out Helen's name, whipping the crowd into a final frenzy.

Helen stands, flexing her biceps.

"Mommy knows best! Mommy knows best! Mommy knows best!" the audience chants even louder than before.

Nikolas ruffles his feathers. "What an amazing victory for Helen Stronghorn."

"But an even better showing for Fauna." I can't help but clap. "She may have lost the match, but she gave the champ a run for her money."

Chapter 14

Lena

"Hey." Daphne approaches me in the locker room, a sheepish smile on her face. "I appreciate you going the extra mile to sell my hits out there."

"No problem!" I clap her on the shoulder. "I'm happy to help a wrestler get the recognition they deserve."

She beams at me. "Hopefully they'll let me win the next one."

"I would be surprised if they didn't. The crowd loved you today."

Straightening her back and standing tall, Daphne oozes confidence. "Thanks again, Lena." She turns to exit the locker room but pauses, looking back at me. "Tell Iris I said hi."

"I wi—I mean…wait…what?"

"Don't play dumb. It's doesn't become you," she says with a wink before exiting the locker room, her goat tail swishing.

What the heck? She's Iris's friend, not mine. What makes Daphne think I'll see Iris first? A pang in my chest reminds me that I likely won't see her until our next rehearsal in a few days. Since when do I care if I get to see Iris or not? How can I get over this weird new feeling?

I know! When I get home tomorrow, I'll call June and Gianna, and we'll go out. Maybe I can hook up with a stranger or something. That kind of reckless behavior would ruin my perfect image if fans found out, but it would be the perfect distraction from Iris. I mean,

I know wrestlers who get away with random hookups. And even if it comes down to a little bad PR, I'll take that over agonizing over Iris.

With a pep in my step, I rush to finish freshening up so I can get plenty of rest before my flight tomorrow morning.

Neither June nor Gianna performed last night, so there's a small chance they may not even be home, spending their off time out on the town. I pick up the phone and try Gianna first. She's more of a homebody than June. A grin spreads across my face as I picture my wolven friend, probably on the couch with a glass of wine and some reality TV show.

After three rings, Gianna's voice answers, "We were wondering if you were going to call."

"We?"

"Yeah. June is over. We're watching some human dating show."

"Thank the goddess you're together. I was wondering if you want to go out tonight?"

Gianna groans. "But we're already comfy. Why don't you just come over and join us?"

"Because I need to get out," I whine.

"Name me something you can do at a bar that you can't do over here, besides spend way too much money on a craft cocktail?"

"Kiss a stranger."

There's a long pause, but I can still hear the TV noise in the background.

"What?" my friend finally breaks the silence. "Since when do you want to kiss strangers? That's ridiculous. Your dad would be pissed if you did that and the media found out."

"I don't care right now. Come on, Gi. Please?" I bat my eyelashes for good measure, even if she can't see me.

"Is this about Iris?"

I scoff. "What makes you say that?"

"I'm not an idiot." Gianna rolls her eyes. "Look, if you want to see her, just call her. I'm sure she wouldn't oppose."

I rub a curl between my forefinger and thumb. "But she said she didn't think we needed to hang out anymore," I respond quietly.

"Ha!" Gianna's triumph is so loud that I pull the receiver away from my ear. "I *knew* this was about Iris!"

"Gi!"

"Hey, June!" she calls, her voice distant. She must have moved the receiver so she could shout to our friend. "We were right, Lena has a crush on Iris."

June squeals. "About time she *finally* admitted it."

"I do not have a crush on Iris!" I argue through gritted teeth.

"Whatever you say," Gianna says, the smile evident in her voice.

"You two are being immature. Crushes? Come on! I'm too old for that crap."

She scoffs. "No, you're not. But if you want us to be more 'mature,' then we'll say you have feelings for her."

I sigh, and rub the bridge of my snout. "I don't have feelings for Iris."

"Lena." Gianna's voice is firm. "Don't lie to us. We're your friends."

"You sure aren't acting like it right now," I snap.

Now it's her turn to sigh. "I'm going to hang up this phone now. The way I see it, you have two options. One: you can go home and pout. Or two: you can call Iris and ask to see her."

"What about option three: us all going out?"

The sound of muffled shuffling fills my ears.

"Lena!" June's bright voice greets me. "Grow up, and tell her how you feel. But if you want to be a reckless twat and make out with a stranger, be my guest. We just aren't going to enable you. Ta-ta."

The phone make a distinct click as she hangs up.

With a groan, I slam the receiver into its holder. How dare my friends accuse me of having feelings for Iris? That's the most ridiculous thing I've ever heard. And I grew up with Charlie Palmer, the king of ridiculous ideas.

Maybe I can just go out by myself. I'm Helen Stronghorn. I'll easily make a friend or two. I bet I could even hook up with them if I wanted to. That will take my mind off Iris.

I pause. But will it, though? I haven't stopped thinking about her, especially since our painting night.

Wait. My painting. Iris never brought it to me.

A large grin spreads across my face.

My fist hovers over Iris's door, ready to knock. Where did my confidence go? I was so sure of myself on the commute to her place, but now that I'm here, I'm hesitating. What if she's not home? Or worse, what if she's pissed I showed up unannounced?

The sound of music is faint, but it's definitely coming from the other side of Iris's door. She's home. I just have to find the courage to knock. I inhale then rap my knuckles against the cool metal.

No going back now. I'm just here to grab my painting. Nothing more.

The music's volume lowers, and the door flings open to reveal Iris, her lower lip between her teeth. "Lena?"

I shuffle from hoof to hoof, even more nervous now that Iris is standing before me. And damn, does she look good. Her long hair is piled on top of her head in a carefree bun, accentuating the curve of her neck. A thin, black tank does nothing to hide her shapely breasts, and matching shorts sit low on her hips.

Iris quirks an eyebrow when I finally drag my gaze to meet hers. Oh shit. She caught me checking her out.

I glance away, focusing my attention on a spot of chipped paint on the wall outside her apartment. "I...uh... Are you busy?"

"No." Iris crosses her arms and leans against the doorframe.

"Cool."

Cool? What the heck kind of response is that? I sound like an idiot.

"Right," she says, drawing out the word. "I hope this doesn't sound rude, but what are you doing here?"

My cheeks and neck flush. I open my mouth to reply, but nothing comes out. Damn Gianna and June for teasing me about my feelings for Iris. Now it's beyond awkward.

I swallow. "Well, I was hoping to get my painting. You never brought it like you promised." Nerves make my voice wobble.

Her lips part as she stares at me. Does she want me to say more? Was this a mistake? I shouldn't have shown up without calling first, but I wanted—no, needed, to see her.

I take a step back, ready to bolt, just as Iris opens her door wider. "Sure. Yeah. Umm…do you want to come in while I grab it real quick?"

"I can stay out here."

Iris shakes her head. "Please stop being weird, and get in here."

Holding the door open wider, Iris motions for me to come inside. I bite my lower lip and step through the doorway into her cozy apartment. A paperback novel lays spread open, pages down on her coffee table next to a plate of cookies.

"What are you reading?" I ask, nodding toward the book.

Iris waves a dismissive hand. "Just a romance novel."

My mouth goes dry. "Oh."

Iris reads romance novels? I don't know why this surprises me. The idea also gets my heart racing. There's one thing I know about romance novels…they can get pretty steamy. Does the book on her coffee table fit the bill?

"Let me grab you a tote or something so it doesn't get damaged," Iris offers, already digging through her closet. After a few moments, she holds up a large black canvas bag. "Found one!"

"That's very kind of you."

Iris slides my painting into the bag. "You worked really hard on this, and it's beautiful. I would hate for something to happen to it."

I take the bag from her with a small smile. "I'm sorry for dropping in without calling first."

"It's alright." She looks down at her feet. "Honestly, it was nice surprise."

"Really?" My ears perk up.

Iris's cheeks darken. "Yeah. I mean, I hate to admit this, but I had a lot of fun with you during our paint party."

"Me too." I can't help it. My voice has gone soft.

When her gaze catches mine again, they shine with something I've never seen in her before.

It looks like hope.

I suck in a deep breath, bracing myself. "What if I stayed?"

Iris's lips part, and her eyebrows lift. "Stayed?"

"Yeah. I mean, maybe we could watch a movie or something?" I clutch the tote against my chest, preparing for rejection.

Her posture relaxes. "I would like that." A large grin overtakes Iris's features.

My heart skips a beat. *Fuck.* She's so beautiful. The idea of spending time with me made her smile like this? Now I'm racking my brain, thinking of all the ways I can get her to look at me like that again. I would do anything to be the cause of that smile.

Oh, motherfucker. Gianna and June are right. I have feelings for Iris.

Her smile drops. "Are you okay? You don't have to hang out with me, you know?"

"That's not it." I shake my head. "Not at all."

Iris chews her lower lip. "Then why do you look like you've seen a ghost?"

I take a step forward, close enough that I can smell her scent of fresh-cut flowers and rain. "Because I…" But I cut myself off.

How do I even begin to express how I feel about her? It's wishful thinking to imagine she would feel the same way, but Gianna and June told me to be honest with her. Iris is owed that, at least. But, damn, my heart is pounding so hard, I can hear it in my ears.

"What is it?" Her question is a whisper, as if fears the answer.

I open my mouth to speak, but I can't find the words.

What am I doing? I'm such a fool. Just tell her.

But I don't.

Instead, I drop the tote and step toward her, closing the small gap between us. Grabbing her by the face, I bend down until my forehead rests against hers.

"L—Lena?" Iris stammers, trembling against me, her wings twitching.

"Please, Iris. Let me kiss you." My heart hammers in my chest and roars in my ears.

She gasps but doesn't pull away. "You want to kiss me?"

"More than anything."

"Then kiss me," she says with a sigh.

And I do.

Chapter 15

Iris

Lena is kissing me. I've never kissed someone with a muzzle before, but I have no problem adjusting. It's tender and hesitant, her hands gently cupping my face. Her hair is soft and silky between my fingers, and I want nothing more than to mess up her perfect curls.

My heart's been pounding ever since she arrived unannounced, but now I fear it may beat out of my chest. I need more of her. More of her kisses, more of her body against mine, just more Lena.

With a light flap of my wings, I propel myself up to be closer to her, her cinnamon and vanilla scent enveloping me. She sucks in a sharp breath, moving her hands from my face to grip my hips. I wrap my legs around her waist, pressing my pelvis against her hard stomach. That prompts a low groan, and she deepens her kiss, parting her lips so I can caress her rough tongue with my own.

When I nip her lower lip, she breaks our kiss. "Iris, fuck. I…"

I run my fingers through her curls, loving the way they spring back into place. "Is this too much?"

Lena grins, shaking her head. "I just never thought I would be so turned on by Iris of the Harpy Clan."

"I thought the same thing about you," I admit with a giggle. "But if you want to stop, we can."

"Wouldn't dream of it," she growls before bringing her mouth to mine again.

Her kiss is demanding now, her mouth parting mine. As our tongues dance, I press against her, craving the friction her rock-hard abs give me. Lena digs her fingers into my hips, almost hard enough to hurt. She's holding back with me, but I'm a professional wrestler. I'm used to pain.

To encourage her, I fist her hair at the roots. Lena lets out a hiss but squeezes me tighter against her, moving her hands from my hips to my ass. Her fingers dig into my flesh.

"Lena," I moan against her mouth.

"Are you trying to drive me crazy?" Lena says, panting.

I flick my tongue over her lips, teasing her. "Is it working?"

"Yes."

"Prove it."

"How far can I go?"

"As far as you're comfortable."

"You're so irritating." Her teeth graze over my bottom lip.

"You love it," I whisper.

Lena smiles against my mouth and begins to walk toward my bed with my legs still wrapped around her waist. When we reach the edge, she lowers me to the mattress and stands above me, her eyes scanning my body.

I curl my finger, beckoning her to me. Lena grins as she lowers herself onto the bed, spreading my legs to fit one of her muscular and massive quads between them. Bringing her mouth to mine, she kisses me, desperate and deep.

One of her hands slips under the hem of my tank top, grazing my stomach. I shiver at the contact, my feathers ruffling.

"I love how your body reacts to my touch," Lena murmurs.

I glide a hand down her cheek and jaw to her chest before teasing one of her breasts over the top of her long-sleeve EMW shirt. Her breath hitches and she thrusts forward, the leg between my thighs creating a delicious friction. I can't help the moan that tumbles from my lips.

Lena brings her mouth to my ear. "I think that's the sexiest sound I've ever heard."

I choke on a laugh and roll my eyes. "You can't be serious."

She hums, bringing the hand she has on my stomach up to one of my breasts.

A gasp escapes me as she brushes her thumb over my nipple. I didn't wear a bra—I wasn't expecting company—and I could kiss my past self right now. My nipple pebbles as Lena rolls it between her forefinger and thumb, and I let out a soft mewl.

Lena nibbles my ear as she continues to work my nipple. I jerk when she gives it a pinch.

"Did I hurt you?" She pulls back so she can look into my eyes.

"Not at all." I smile. "You're so sweet for asking, but I don't want sweet right now."

Her eyes take on a mischievous glint. "Oh yeah? What do you want, Iris?"

I respond by grinding against her leg.

"You're a greedy one, aren't you?" Lena looks at me as if she's starving and I'm a fresh slice of cake, ready to be devoured.

Lena adjusts the leg between my thighs so that her knee is pressed against my hot and throbbing cunt. Her hand on my breast continues to play with my nipple while she uses the other to keep herself propped up, her gaze fixed on me. She rubs her knee against my pussy, a smile on her face. She looks so damn satisfied.

"Oh fuck," I moan, thrusting against her knee.

Thank the goddess the fabric of my shorts is thin, otherwise I'm not sure I'd feel the texture of her fur against my aching clit; and it feels amazing.

"I can feel how wet you are through your shorts, Iris." She matches the rhythm of my hip thrusts with her circling knee, which gives me extra sensation.

"Lena!" I cry out.

She lets out a low hum. "I like it when you say my name like that."

My hands find her rippling biceps, the fingertips digging into the muscles as I continue to grind against her. I arch my hips, let my head fall back, and close my eyes.

A rough hand grabs my ass, stilling my race to my climax. I let out a frustrated whine, my eyes snapping open to glare at Lena.

"That's right, don't close your eyes on me. I want to see that pretty face come undone. Don't close your eyes on me, baby girl."

"Goddess. You're the worst," I groan, but I oblige nonetheless, keeping my gaze locked with hers.

Lena smirks. "Is that right?" She moves her knee away from my pussy. "Should I stop, then?"

"Don't you dare!" I growl, pulling her back to me.

She falls forward, catching herself with the hand that was on my hip. "Greedy," she huffs but begins rubbing herself against me again.

I thrust harder than before. There's something sexy about the way Lena's gaze is trained on my face. What is it about this minotaur that makes me so hot? I hated her a few weeks ago, and now I'm dry humping her, quickly approaching orgasm.

"That's it, Iris." Lena gives my breast a rough squeeze. "Use me to get off."

"Lena!" I whine. "I'm close."

"Say my name as you come."

And that's all it takes. I roll my hips and my breathing becomes more erratic. "Lena! I'm coming!"

"That's it," she purrs. "Come on me."

My vision goes blurry as I reach my peak, but I don't take my eyes off Lena, even if her beautiful face goes out of focus. I dig my nails into her arms, positive that if she didn't have fur, I would leave marks on her skin.

I collapse, legs spread wide as I come down from my orgasm. Fuck. That was the hottest moment of my life and all I did was dry hump her leg like I was a horny teenager again.

"Oh, goddess," I groan, covering my face with my arm.

Lena takes my wrist and moves my arm. "Why are you hiding from me?"

"Because I just got off grinding myself against your leg."

She laughs "It was hot."

I tilt my head. "Really?"

"Do you want to find out just how hot I thought it was?" Lena asks, her gaze heavy.

I lick my lips. "You know I do."

She takes one of my hands currently resting on her biceps and drags it down her body to the elastic waistband of her athletic shorts. With an adjustment of my wrist, I assist her in getting my hand down the front of her shorts and panties.

My fingers graze her entrance. She's already wet. She shivers above me, and I can't help the wicked smile that forms on my lips. All of this? For me?

I slip a thumb between her folds, gathering her arousal before sliding up to her clit.

"Iris!" Lena hisses. "That feels…"

"Good?"

She manages to glare at me. "You know it does."

I smirk and continue working her clit. There's something thrilling about being the one to pleasure this large and sexy minotaur. Her eyelids flutter as I increase the pressure on her sensitive nub. I have half a mind to exact payback from her—tell her to look at me as she comes—but I want her to fully enjoy herself. Besides, this angle is perfect.

Once Lena closes her eyes and throws her head back in a loud moan, I adjust my hand so I can slip a finger inside her. She's tight, wet, and hot around me, and I'm quickly becoming aroused again.

"Oh fuck," she whines. "Give me more."

"And I'm the greedy one?" I slide another finger inside.

Her eyes narrow. "Shut up!"

"Oh, I don't think I will." I curl my fingers to hit her G-spot. "How's that?"

Lena hums in response.

"Talk to me, pretty girl."

"It feels good, Iris," she moans.

"How do my fingers feel inside you?" I ask as I begin to thrust my fingers in and out of her soaked pussy.

"I want more."

"More?"

"Please."

"Since you asked so nicely."

I do as she's requested and slip a third finger inside her tight cunt. Lena groans and begins rolling her hips. I adjust my hand again, so I fuck her with my three fingers while rubbing her clit with the heel of my hand.

"Fuck, Iris. That feels incredible," she says in between heavy breaths.

Lena's arms begin to quake. But she's too strong to be shaking like this. She must be getting close. To encourage her over the edge, I slide my unoccupied hand up her shirt and under her bra to stroke her nipple. She shudders at my touch.

I increase the pace of my fingers. "Are you going to come for me, pretty girl?"

She nods, her curls shimmering in the dim light of the lamp on my bedside table.

"Answer me," I demand along with a pinch of her nipple.

"Oh fuck, yes! I'm close!"

"I want to feel that tight cunt come around my fingers. Would you like that?"

"Oh, goddess, yes. I want to come so bad."

I make sure she can see my grin and then slide in my pinkie, stretching her even more.

"Iris!" Lena moans.

Her eyes squeeze shut, her tongue pokes out between parted lips, and her fists clench my sheets. She's so hot, her strong biceps bulging and her beautiful face twisted in pleasure. I gasp when her whole torso clenches, turned on by how her cunt flutters around my fingers. She's downright exquisite when she comes.

Lena sighs, and she relaxes. I slide my fingers out of her pussy and roll her onto her back so she can go limp without the worry of collapsing on me and crushing me. Not that she would hurt me, but I don't want her to be concerned for my comfort. This is her moment.

I lie next to her, peppering her face and neck with soft kisses. She hums, snuggling into me.

Lena laces a hand in one of mine and brings it to her lips, pressing a kiss to each knuckle. "That was… I have no words for how incredible that was."

"I can't believe we did that."

She stiffens. "Do you regret it?"

I adjust so I can look into her big brown eyes. "Not at all. It's just a little wild that we went from hating each other to making each other come."

Lena laughs. "You're right. It's a little bonkers."

"But in a good way."

We stare at each other with small, satisfied grins. The silence is comfortable and cozy. My eyes begin to grow heavy, Lena's body heat lulling me to the edge of sleep.

"Hey, Iris?" Lena's soft question cuts through the silence.

"What's up?" I don't bother opening my eyes.

"Would you tell me what it is about the audience that upsets you?"

I don't know if it's the fact that I'm gooey from my orgasm or the fact that I feel safe with Lena, or maybe a combination of both, but the answer flows from me without hesitation. "I hate that they boo me."

She gasps. Really?"

"I'm forced to play a heel." I finally open my eyes to look at Lena. "And I hate it."

A frown mars her perfect face.

"It's okay," I add. "I should be used to it by now."

"It's not okay." She shakes her head. "If you don't want to play the heel, you shouldn't have to."

I take her hand in mine. "It's not that easy. Especially for someone like me. I don't have any kind of influence over Mr. Palmer."

"It should be easier," she mumbles. "You're just as good of a wrestler as me."

"Please don't dwell on it." I bring her hand to my lips and kiss her knuckles. "I just want us to be here, in this moment. Forget about work for a while."

I find myself biting my lower lip. "You don't have to, if you don't want to, but I have tomorrow off, and I assume you do too. Maybe we can spend the day together?"

Lena's smile is bright, her brown eyes shining in the dark. "Sounds perfect to me."

I angle my face so I can capture her mouth with mine. Our kiss is soft and sweet, all the demands and desperation replaced with comfort and satisfaction.

"Goodnight, Iris," Lena whispers, breaking our kiss but pulling me tight against her.

"Goodnight, Lena."

Commercial Break

Never Stand On A Swivel Chair

The cloven hoof of a satyr with brown fur steps onto a chair cushion, his hands gripping the arm rests to hold himself steady. When he places his other hoof onto the seat, he wobbles, unsure on his feet. The camera zooms out to reveal the satyr is standing on a swivel office chair as he reaches for a framed photo of his family on the wall.

His mouth forms a perfect *O*, and his eyes flash with fear when he stands straight up. His arms flail, and he begins falling in slow motion as dramatic music plays. The camera zooms on his face, the fear evident in his hazel eyes.

The shot cuts to Eileen Waterclaw dressed in a blue windowpane suit jacket and pencil skirt, standing in the foreground of the scene as the satyr continues to fall in slow motion. Suddenly, the footage switches to normal speed, just as the satyr crashes to the ground. Behind Eileen, he writhes in pain, clutching his back.

A concerned look crosses the dragon's face. "Not everyone can take a fall like I can, and that's why you should be safe and never stand on a swivel chair."

The satyr continues to roll around on the ground. Eileen glances at him over her shoulder and turns back around to face the camera, shaking her head.

"This message is brought to you by the United Stepstool and Ladder Association," she says with a small smile as the logo for the USALA pops up on the bottom of the screen.

Chapter 16

Iris

I GROAN AS I ROLL out of bed before stretching my wings and arms wide. "I'm so sore."

Lena snickers, eyes still closed. "Good."

I try to glare, but a smile curves on my lips instead. "Good?"

"Yeah." She sits up and drags me onto her lap. "It means I fucked you good today."

Heat creeps up my face and neck. Lena's not wrong. "Maybe it's because we had a nonstop sex marathon."

"Are you saying I didn't fuck you good?" She waggles her eyebrows.

"I mean, you did." I don't tell her that it was the best sex of my life. "But I thought maybe we would have more cuddling. Maybe watch a movie or two."

"Don't tell me you wish we had watched a movie instead of experiencing my tongue between your legs multiple times?"

I shake my head. "That's not what I said. I'm...glad you came over last night. I'm just feeling it now is all."

A large grin spreads across Lena's face as her tail wraps around my ankle. "I'm glad I came over, too."

"So, it was good for you, too?"

"Good?" Her ears twitch. "It was amazing, if I'm being honest."

She pops a kiss on my cheek. "I should probably get going, though."

My heart sinks. "Why?"

"Because we have to train tomorrow, and if I stay here, I'll just want to eat that delicious pussy of yours all night instead of sleeping. Besides, I need to grab fresh clothes."

I run my fingers through her curls. After a day of rolling around in the bed, I'm proud to say they are a mess rather than perfectly coiled. "And you should probably take care of this sex hair."

Lena laughs and rubs a lock of my hair between her forefinger and thumb. "You're one to talk."

"So we both need to take care of our hair." I laugh, standing to allow her to get off the bed.

Grabbing her discarded shorts and shirt, she begins to dress. "I hate our rigorous schedule sometimes."

"Me, too." I sigh. "But it's worth it to live the dream."

Lena nods with a smile. "Agreed."

"Do you want a snack before you go?" I ask, waving at the kitchen.

"If I eat another Pop Tart, I'm going to barf." she says, rubbing her stomach. "Come to my place for our next hangout, and I'll make sure we have home-cooked meals to give us plenty of energy."

I playfully roll my eyes. "You seemed to run just fine on my junk food, thank you very much."

"I powered through for you." Lena leans down and kisses me, bringing her hand to my face.

Her warm scent of cinnamon and vanilla barely clings to her skin, mixing with my perfume and our sweat. It's a fantastic smell, and it's a shame I can't bottle it.

I break our kiss, as much as I hate to. What I really want to do is drag her back to bed, but she's right. It's time we have a little break so we can get back to work tomorrow.

Lena takes one last look at me, her gaze lingering on my mouth, before releasing from our embrace and exiting my apartment. I release a happy hum when the door closes behind her, one of the best days of my life coming to an end.

Dragging myself to my extra deep and wide tub to accommodate my wings, I draw myself the hottest bath I can manage and sink in. The scalding water feels like heaven around my aching muscles. I've never felt like this after sex before, and I can't wait until next time.

Next time.

Lena did mention there would be a next time, so I don't have to worry that this was a onetime thing. If Lena wanted that, I wouldn't protest, but I would be devastated. Not only am I ruined for sex now, but I know now my feelings are more than just sex.

But is that even possible? What would Mr. Palmer say about us dating? We would ruin the illusion that heels and faces don't get along, exposing the scripted aspect of the EMW. He would not stand for that. Honestly, keeping this big secret that we're scripted is getting old. The only time I can really be myself is behind closed doors. I can't even be recognized at the grocery store without having to don my heel persona. It's exhausting.

I sink lower into the tub, blowing bubbles in disappointment. There's no way I'll ever be allowed to date Lena. But I want the world to see me with her, to know she's mine and I'm hers.

But who knows if she even feels the same way? This could be just a friends-with-benefits situation for her. But I would venture to guess it's not. Not after the way she looked at me so tenderly, making me feel cherished. I guess I'll have to take a risk and ask her how she feels.

My heart begins to hammer against my rib cage. I'm now both looking forward to seeing Lena tomorrow and dreading it.

I arrive at the EMW's gym early, even for me. The idea is that if I do enough cardio, I'll be more tired than anxious, making it easier to confront Lena. We're supposed to be running through a few of the bigger moves today and planning our finisher, so I need to be completely focused.

Setting the treadmill at a brutal speed and hitting *Play* on my portable CD player, I begin my run. Heavy metal music always gets me pumped up, and I lose myself in the thrashing guitars as I concentrate on my breathing and posture rather than Lena and her enticing curves.

A soft touch on my shoulder shocks me out of my focus.

What the fuck was that?

I nearly stumble on the treadmill, instead taking to the air to avoid smashing my face. Ripping my earbuds out, I look around the gym, frantic to find who or what touched me.

"Whoa! Iris! I'm so sorry. I didn't mean to scare you," Lena says from behind me.

"Lena!" I clutch my chest over my pounding heart and float back down to the floor. "I didn't hear you come in."

She offers me a tentative smile. "I was trying to grab your attention, but I think your music was too loud or something and you couldn't hear me."

I punch the buttons on the treadmill, bringing it to a stop. "Sorry. That's my bad. I was just super focused."

She giggles "I can tell."

But I can't think of anything witty or fun to say back to her. Despite my best efforts to tire myself out, I'm still nervous.

"What's wrong?" Lena asks, crossing her arms.

I take a step back. "What makes you think something is wrong?"

She scoffs. "I've spent years watching you, and the last few weeks becoming your friend. You don't think I know when something is up?"

My stomach swoops. "You spent years watching me?"

"Well…" Lena glances at the floor. "Yeah. I probably spent too much time glaring at you. But I'm realizing now that it may have been attraction. I just hadn't figured it out yet."

I waggle my eyebrows. "Really?"

She looks up at me with a grin. "Yeah. Really."

We stand there, smiling at each other like two goofballs. I'm afraid to break the comfortable silence, but I need to confront her about how I feel.

I clear my throat. "Can I talk to you about something?"

Lena's happy expression falters. "Are you regretting what we did?"

"No. Not at all." I step forward and rest my hand on her biceps. "The opposite, actually."

"What do you mean?"

I chew my lower lip. How am I going to say this? I should have practiced or something.

"Where do you see this going?" I finally blurt out the question, and it's loud, echoing off the gym walls.

"Wherever you'll let it go," she responds in a soft and vulnerable tone.

"What do you mean?" I cock my head, my wings flexing in anticipation.

Lena cups my cheek. "Whatever you want, I want. If that means nothing more than friendship, I'll be happy. As long as you're in my life."

"What if I told you I want everything?" My voice quivers.

She sucks in a breath. "Everything?"

I nuzzle my cheek into her hand and kiss her palm. "I want all of you."

Her face softens. "And I want all of you."

"It's not just sex for you?"

"Is that what you were worried about?" Lena tilts my chin up.

I nod.

Lena leans down to capture my lips. "It's not just sex," she murmurs.

"Good." My heart is soaring. "Even though the sex is amazing."

Her eyes gleam. "Oh yeah?"

"I'm *still* a little sore. All those orgasms worked my entire body."

She laughs. "Too bad I have to slam you around now."

"Don't threaten me with a good time," I say with a wink.

With another laugh, Lena drags me to the ring. "Let's talk how to get into position for the top rope suplex."

"Alright." I climb the ropes and sit on the top turnbuckle. "Do you think you should be here, getting ready to do an elbow drop or something?"

Lena nods, approaching me. "Yeah. Maybe I would have just done a facebuster, and you're lying there. Of course, I'm celebrating and basking in my awesomeness. The audience will think this is the end."

I nod. "Yes! While you're distracted with the crowd, I'll crawl up the top ropes and start chopping you across the chest."

With a wicked grin, Lena climbs the rope until she's face to face with me. "Like this?"

"Yes." I chortle. "But don't chop me right now. That shit hurts."

"Maybe I'll just smother you with my mouth instead." She trails a finger over my lips.

"If only," I say with a wistful sigh.

"No harm in practicing." Lena shrugs before bringing her lips to my neck.

I gasp. "Lena! We're at the gym."

"Yeah." She continues to kiss and nip at the delicate skin. "And no one should be arriving for another half hour. That's plenty of time."

I cock my head. "Plenty of time for what?"

Lena hops down one rope so she's at eye level with my hips. "This." She tugs at my shorts.

I bite back a groan. "You can't be serious. I'm all sweaty." But I'm already wet.

She stops pulling on my shorts and points at her face. Her brows are furrowed and she's frowning. "Do I look like I'm fucking around here?"

"Nope." I laugh in disbelief. *Are we really doing this?*

"Good," Lena grunts. "Now, stop being so difficult, and take these shorts off."

I lift my hips to give her better access to finish undressing me. The gym air is cool against my skin, but the rest of me feels flushed as her breath ghosts over my bare thighs. Lena grabs my legs and urges them apart.

When my legs fall open, she lets out a chuckle. "You're already wet for me, I see."

My cheeks grow hot. "I can't help what you do to me."

Lena begins kissing my thighs, working her way closer to my throbbing pussy. Her nose grazes my entrance, and I tense.

"Relax," she demands.

But the moment I do, she drags her tongue from entrance to clit in one long stroke. The rough texture of her tongue against my sensitive clit is earth-shatteringly good. Something about the potential of getting caught gives the act a new and dangerous element.

"You taste sensational." Lena groans against my pussy. "I can't get enough of you."

She licks me again, this time ending the stroke by circling my clit. I moan, gripping the top rope with my hands and my talons. Fuck! It feels amazing.

And Lena is not wasting a moment in pushing me toward climax. She knows my body by now, and what I like. On our first night together, she took her time, savoring each moan. But she's eating me now like she hasn't tasted food in days.

"Lena!" I whine, bucking my hips. "I'm getting close."

"I need to feel it, sweetheart. I need every last drop," she growls, moving her mouth to my entrance while her thumb finds my swollen bundle of nerves.

The best thing about Lena's tongue is its width and length. I cry out when she plunges it into my wet cunt. My hands lose their grip on the rope, and I move them to her horns. I use them to set the pace, wanting her to textured tongue fuck me harder and faster. I'm so close. As if knowing exactly what I need, Lena begins stroking my clit with her thumb.

"Oh fuck," I moan, clutching her horns for dear life. "Don't stop!"

Lena begins thrusting her tongue in and out of my pussy with a new vigor, spurring me closer to the edge. I roll my hips, driving my cunt into her face. At this rate, her fur will be soaked in my cum.

The thought of her marked by me sends me over the edge. I throw my head back with a strangled cry. My pussy clenches around her tongue, but she keeps lapping at me, her thumb never ceasing its strokes on my clit. My thighs quake and my vision blurs as the hard and intense orgasm crashes through my body.

By the time I've reached my peak and begun my descent, I'm jelly in Lena's arms. She eases me off the top turnbuckle onto her lap.

"How did that feel, sweetheart?" She runs her fingers through my hair.

"Incredible," I murmur.

I reach for the waistband of her shorts, eager to return the favor, but she brushes my hand away. "Not right now."

"But why?" I'm too tired to hold back my whine.

She smirks. "Not everything has to be reciprocated. Besides, I think I hear someone coming."

I pause and listen. Sure enough, the sounds of muffled voices float into the gym.

"Shit, Lena!" I rush to stand, looking around for my shorts. "Why didn't you tell me sooner?"

Lena brings a hand to her mouth to stifle a laugh.

My eyes narrow. "It's not funny!"

She can't contain her laughter any longer. "It's hilarious!"

I roll my eyes. "Where are my shorts?"

Lena tosses me my shorts and panties, and I fumble to yank them on. I manage to have them settled on my hips just in time for Lucy to walk through the door with another wrestler.

She looks between us, her brows knitted together. "What's going on here? You two aren't fighting again, are you?"

Lena and I glance at each other. I almost got caught with my pants down, literally. Laughter threatens to bubble up my throat. I don't know if it's the endorphins from my orgasm or the ridiculousness of the situation, but I'm giddy.

I bring my hand to my mouth, but it's no use. A guffaw erupts from my mouth as I look over at Lena, who is shaking with silent laughter. Before long, we're both on the mat, clutching our stomachs, and kicking our feet.

Lucy gapes at us. "I don't know if I like you two getting along. It smells like trouble."

Chapter 17

Lena

"Hey," Iris whispers, looking around the locker room. "Do you want to get out of here?"

I smirk. "Your cunt is awfully greedy."

Her cheeks darken. "That's not what I meant."

"Oh?" My ears twitch.

It's been one amazing week since Iris and I hooked up. Exhausting, too, from all the sex, but still easily the best seven days of my life. We haven't had a single argument. Sure, we still bicker, but that's just how we flirt at this point.

And the best part? We've nailed all the big moves in rehearsal, including the finisher.

Lucy was suspicious of our harmonious nature at first, but we've since reassured her that our Charlie-mandated fun time worked. We haven't told anyone we're dating, not even our friends. If the tabloids ever got word, it would shatter the characters Charlie has crafted for us.

Using her wings to shield our faces, Iris huddles closer to me. "Want to get breakfast?"

I wrap my freshly washed hair in a towel. "Sure. I just have to stop at the store and get some bread for toast, but I have everything else we need."

"I'm not talking about making breakfast." She shakes her head. "I meant at the little café around the corner from my apartment."

"And how do you propose we do that?" I ask with a snort.

Iris produces two pairs of large black sunglasses from behind her back, a smirk on her lips. "With these."

"Umm…you do realize we are two of the most recognizable wrestlers in the realm, right?"

"Sure, but maybe if we tie our hair back and wear hats, we could get away with it."

"Let me guess." I place my hands on my hips. "You also already have hats for us?"

"I do!" Iris reveals her other hand, which clutches two black baseball caps.

Embroidered on one hat in white thread are the words *I'M WITH THE TALL CHICK*, while the other says *THE TALL CHICK*.

I laugh. "Are you serious? Iris, this will draw even more attention to us."

She waves me off, shoving the hats and sunglasses in my hands so she can start tying up her hair. "People will just think we're corny tourists. By the way, you're 'the tall chick.' It even has holes in it for your horns."

"Thanks," I respond, deadpan.

"You're welcome." Iris giggles. "Now, hurry up. I'm starving."

While our disguises are awful, her smile and enthusiasm make it so I can't deny her wishes. Besides, I would be lying if I said I didn't want the opportunity to go on a real date with her, instead of hiding out in one of our apartments. I rush to finish getting ready, excited to go on a new adventure with Iris.

"Should we call a car?" I don the hat and sunglasses.

She shakes her head. "Let's give our disguises the ultimate test."

"You don't mean getting on the train, do you?" My jaw hangs open.

"I do!" Iris grabs my hand, leading me out of the locker room. "Let's go."

Usually, if I take public transportation, I'm recognized at least a few times. They whisper to their friends, pointing at me. Some are even brave enough to approach me. But not today. Instead, people barely spare me a passing glance. Some give us a second look, but it's probably the stupid hats we're wearing.

I relax during our commute, inching closer and closer to Iris on the train. By the time we reach our stop, we're even holding hands. A thrill runs through me at this public display of affection—yes, because it's risky, but also because I'm proud to have Iris on my arm. She's gorgeous, funny, smart, and hardworking, and her wingspan is impressive. I couldn't ask for a better girlfriend.

When we reach the café, Iris requests to sit on the patio. Perfect. We can keep our hats and sunglasses on this way. The human server who takes our drink order eyes us, but, again, I'm blaming the hats.

"We're actually getting away with this!" Iris squeals after the server has poured our coffee and walked away.

I shake my head. "I don't know how."

She points at her hat. "All thanks to our disguises."

"This is insane," I say with a smile.

"But you're enjoying yourself." Iris nudges me with her elbow. "Besides, I thought you were the adventurous one, Miss Eat-Out-Your-Girlfriend-At-The-Gym."

I laugh. "That was worth it."

She cocks her head. "And this isn't?"

"Any moment I have with you is worth it," I whisper, leaning in to pop a kiss on the top of her head over her hat. I can't exactly kiss her on the cheek with these ridiculous hats and sunglasses on.

"What are you ordering?" Iris murmurs, her cheeks flushing that lovely shade of blue gray that indicates she's flustered.

"I think I'm going to go for a mess of scrambled eggs and a fat stack of pancakes. You?"

She points to the menu. "Eggs, of course, and they have a giant cinnamon roll that I've been wanting to try."

"Hot sauce for your eggs?"

She smiles, flashing her fangs. "Of course."

My tail swishes, and I can't help but beam and puff out my chest. I've done my best to learn everything I can about Iris, and it feels awesome to apply that knowledge outside our apartments.

"Oh!" She folds her menu closed. "I have one request for this date."

I sit up straight. "What's that?"

"No work talk. This is our first outing together, and I don't want to spoil it."

"Of course." I nod. "Whatever you want."

The server returns. "Are you ready to order?"

We nod and place our breakfast orders. When the server is out of earshot, I turn back to Iris. "What do you want to talk about?"

She puts her elbows on the table and laces her fingers under her chin. "If you could be anything in the world, other than a wrestler, what would you be?"

I let out a long whistle. "I never really thought about it. I can't remember a time when wrestling wasn't my first career choice. Having a backup never really occurred to me because my dad never encouraged me to have one. It was always assumed I would get a main roster spot one day."

"But what about now? You're an adult with your own passions and hobbies outside wrestling, right?"

"Hmmm…" I rub my chin. "Probably something to do with food. I love to cook, and I like to think I'm pretty decent at it."

"Decent?" Iris gasps. "You're an amazing cook. I can see it now… You in a chef hat and apron, ordering around a busy kitchen. Monsters and humans alike would come from all over just to taste your food."

I cackle with laughter. "That's a fun idea. But cooking for just you is fun, too. What about you? What would you want to do?"

"Probably write books," she blurts out before dropping her gaze to the table.

"That's so cool. I think you would be really good at that."

Iris catches my eye, her cheeks flushed and her eyes shining. "Really?"

"Yeah." I reach out and begin to twirl the end of her ponytail between my fingers. "You're so creative and funny. I would love to read anything you write."

She scoffs. "You're just saying that because you're my girlfriend."

"I'm not."

"Sure." She crosses her arms over her chest. "But I appreciate your support."

I shake my head. "You don't trust me to be honest with you?"

Her features soften. "I do trust you."

At that moment, the server returns with a tray, our breakfasts balanced on top. "Here you go." They smile as they place our plates on the table. "Can I get you anything else?"

Iris and I shake our heads and thank the server. The food is delicious. Not as good as mine, but it still hits the spot after a grueling training session.

It's a wonderful experience being out in public with Iris. It's like we're a normal couple and not two of the most famous monsters in the realm who are scheduled to fight each other at the biggest wrestling event of the year.

If only we could do this without the disguises.

I'm deep in thought about Iris's and my relationship one evening while Iris and I snuggle on her couch, dressed in plush bathrobes, a plate of cookies on our laps. She can't cook, but it turns out she can make an excellent chocolate chip cookie.

"What are you thinking about?" Iris asks, interrupting my thoughts.

My cheeks heat. "Oh. It's nothing."

Iris frowns. "Doesn't seem like nothing."

"It's just…" I sigh. "I love that we've been going on dates and spending all this time together…"

"But?"

"But I hate sneaking around."

"Oh." Her throat bobs. "Do you want to call it quits?"

"Are you kidding me?" I pull her tighter against me. "And miss out on your cookies? No way!"

She clutches her chest, a fake pout on her lips. "Is that all I am to you? A cookie?"

I shrug, but I can't stop the corners of my mouth from lifting. "Maybe I need a reminder of what your other coo—"

A knock on the door startles us both.

"Were you expecting company?" I ask, whispering.

"No." The response is more of a question than an answer.

"Come on, Iris!" a familiar voice calls from the other side of the door. "We know you're in there!"

"Oh shit!" Iris stands up. "It's Daphne. And Pan must be with her."

"Do they still think we're doing mandated fun time?"

"I'm not sure." She sighs. "I guess there's only one way to find out."

"Right."

When Iris opens the door, sure enough, Daphne and Pan are on the other side, wide smiles plastered on their faces. Both are dressed in casual sweats. Daphne clutches a bottle of wine while Pan has a brown paper bag of what smells like takeout from a Naga restaurant. Their jaws drop when they see me.

"Lena?" Daphne blinks as if clearing her eyes.

Iris lets out a cough. "Yeah. Just a little 'mandated fun time' from Mr. Palmer."

Pan quirks an eyebrow. "In your matching bathrobes?"

Daphne huffs. "And you used to always call us to bitch about spending time with Lena. But we haven't heard about her in a while."

"Oh!" Iris glances back at me. "Everything is fine now. Ha! Guess Mr. Palmer was right. We just needed to spend some time together."

I nod. "Yeap. Just doing what Charlie asked."

Pan flicks their red demon tail. "I hate to ask again, *but in your matching bathrobes?"*

Iris pales. "We...didn't... I mean—"

Daphne lets out a boisterous laugh and pushes herself into the apartment. "We aren't idiots."

"What do you mean?" Iris asks, eyes wide.

"We know you two are fucking," Daphne snorts with a conspiratorial smile on her lips.

Pan follows Daphne, plopping the takeout bag on the counter. "Sorry to drop by unannounced, but we haven't seen you outside of work in what feels like too long. We missed you."

"But now our suspicions as to why have been confirmed." Daphne shoots me a wink. "You're getting that fine minotaur ass."

Iris snaps her wings. "Daph!"

"What?" Daphne cocks her head. "Am I wrong?"

"No, but…" Iris's blush creeps down her neck.

Daphne pats her on the shoulder, her goat tail wagging. "You know I can't help teasing you."

Pan begins rifling through the cabinet, pulling out plates and wineglasses. "I hope you don't mind us crashing your date."

I rise from the couch. "Yeah. Sorry. I'm in the way. I'll let you three have a friend night."

"No!" Daphne and Pan shout in unison.

Daphne places a hand on my shoulder "We would love to get to know you better."

Pan agrees with a nod. "Who is the woman occupying all our friend's time?"

"Exactly." Daphne clicks her tongue. "We aim to find out."

I swish my tail. "Are you sure?"

"Yes," Daphne says with an assured grin.

Iris crosses her arms over her chest. "I like how you two didn't ask me at all."

Pan tucks a lock of their black bob behind their ear. "We apologized."

"Sure did." Daphne uncorks the bottle of wine. "Don't you miss us?"

Iris relaxes, a soft smile on her lips. "I do." She looks at me and mouths, *Is this okay?*

I approach her and take her in my arms, planting a kiss on her lips. "It's perfect." It feels amazing to show Iris how much I care about her in front of her friends.

Daphne coos. "You two are adorable."

Pan hands me a plate. "Here. There's plenty of food."

"What do we want to watch?" Daphne grabs the remote and plops onto the couch.

"I could go over a romantic comedy," Pan says before shoving a bite of food into their mouth.

"Great! I think the newest enemies-to-lovers one is about to start on the Chick Flick Channel."

"Oh!" Iris's wings quiver. "I've been wanting to watch that one."

Daphne smirks. "You would."

"What's that supposed to mean?"

"Um…hello? It's literally your relationship?"

Iris sticks her tongue out at her friend and settles onto the floor, motioning for me to join her.

Pan looks at me. "I hope you're okay with talking during movies because we basically don't shut up."

I giggle. "Sounds like a good time."

And it is. The movie is bad, but getting to know Pan and Daphne outside work is a treat. I really enjoy their company.

"Oh shit." Daphne points to Pan as the credits roll on the movie. "They're asleep."

And sure enough, Pan is passed out on the couch, face buried in a decorative pillow.

"Are they okay?" I ask, leaning forward to check on them.

"Oh yeah." Daphne giggles. "They always fall asleep like that."

"Should we wake them?"

Daphne glances at Iris, brows pinched.

Iris shakes her head. "Let them sleep."

"Where am I going to sleep?" Daphne asks, perking up.

"I still have a blow-up mattress in my closet," Iris says.

Daphne springs to her hooves. "Fuck yes! Slumber party!"

I grin and help Iris and Daphne set up the mattress. Once everyone is settled and I'm lying in bed, Iris in my arms, it occurs to me that this is my first sleepover with friends.

The scent of frying potatoes wakes me. Pan is standing over the stove, spatula in hand.

"Hey," they whisper when they notice me. "Sorry for waking you."

I peel myself out from underneath Iris, who is still in a deep sleep. Careful not to make too much noise when my hooves clack on the wooden floor, I make my way to Pan.

"Where did you get this food?" I ask. "Iris doesn't exactly have a stocked kitchen."

"I snuck out early this morning and went shopping."

"And we didn't hear you?"

They shrug. "Demon stuff."

I hold back a laugh. "How can I help?"

They wave me off. "You can help by calling June and Gianna?"

"June and Gianna?"

"I don't know their numbers. And I thought, maybe if you were ready for them to know about your relationship with Iris, that we could all have breakfast together."

I tap a finger against my chin. "You know, they're probably in the same boat as you and Daphne were. In fact, they encouraged me to tell Iris how I feel."

Pan shakes their head, a soft smile on their face. "It's so funny you two thought you were being slick."

My blood runs cold. "Do you think everyone else knows?"

They turn to look at me. "Why are you worried?"

"I can't imagine Charlie being thrilled about us dating. I mean, if anyone outside of the EMW found out, it would ruin everything he's built."

"Ah!" Pan stirs the potatoes. "If it makes you feel any better, I think the only reason we knew is because we know Iris so well. We're all best friends, after all. And I'm willing to bet it's the same for June and Gianna."

I let out a long breath. "Let's hope that's the case."

"And you know we won't tell anyone, right? We love Iris and would never do anything to jeopardize her happiness."

"Yeah." I smile. "I trust you."

"Good." Pan grins. "Now, call up your friends. I want there to be plenty of hot breakfast for everyone."

Chapter 18

Iris

"I CAN'T BELIEVE MONSTERMADNESS IS next week." Frowning, I knead Lena's shoulders as she sits on the floor with me on the couch behind her.

She groans when my thumb finds a particularly large knot. "Right there," Lena confirms.

"I know it's not your first time main eventing MonsterMadness, Lena, but it's mine, and I just can't quite wrap my head around it."

The knot dissipates under my efforts and Lena lets out a long, relieved sigh. "You don't sound excited about it." She turns around to look at me. "What's going on?"

"I know I should be thrilled," I admit with a sigh. "But I can't help being disappointed that I'm going to lose. My dream has always been to hold the EMW Realms Championship in my hands."

Lena bites her bottom lip. "I'm sorry."

I shrug. "I really shouldn't be talking to you about this. I don't want to make you uncomfortable. You're the one slated to win."

"Hey," she says, taking my face into her hands, "you can talk to me about anything."

"But it isn't fair to put this on you."

She lets out a deep sigh. "I get to decide what's fair for me and what's not. And I think I'm your girlfriend first, and your opponent at MonsterMadness second."

I beam at her. "You're too good to me."

"Not at all." Lena kisses my nose. "You deserve everything, including that championship."

My smile falters. "Too bad I'll never have it."

"You don't know that."

I roll my eyes. "I've been with the EMW for ten years and I've never held a championship belt."

She tilts her head. "Really? But you're a damn good wrestler."

"But I always lose whenever I challenge for a championship. That's just the way it is for me."

"What the fuck?" Lena growls. "How is it that I've never noticed that Charlie has done that to you?"

I shake my head. "Because I win all my other matches, so I still look like a formidable opponent."

"This is fucked up."

My shoulders slump. "What can I do?"

"Why can't you just ask Charlie to win a championship?" she asks, as if it's the most obvious solution in the realm.

I roll my eyes. "Easy for you to say. You're practically best friends."

Lena runs her fingers through her hair, brushing stray curls away from her face. "He's best friends with my dad, but I get what you're saying." She perks up. "Maybe I can ask him?"

"No!" I make an X with my arms. "No way! You know Mr. Palmer better than that. He would laugh in your face and probably make sure I lose the next ten matches or something for being such a coward."

"You're right." She pouts. "But you're onto something there. He doesn't appreciate cowards. Your best bet is to buck up and ask him."

Deep in thought, I twirl a lock of my hair around my forefinger. Lena has a point. Mr. Palmer might even appreciate me having the guts to ask. "Alright."

"Alright?" Lena smiles. "You'll ask?"

I nod. "I doubt he'll give me the EMW Realms Championship, and definitely not at MonsterMadness, but maybe one of the other titles."

She claps her hands. "Yes! I'm so proud of you."

"I haven't even asked yet," I say, but I can't help the smile that spreads across my face at her enthusiasm. "But I'll probably wait until after MonsterMadness."

"The point is that you will." Lena kisses me. "Let's celebrate!"

I waggle my brows. "Will you sit on my face?"

She laughs. "While I love that idea, I think we should go out tonight."

"Out?" I look at the clock. "But it's already ten at night."

"Exactly."

"That's ridiculous." I shake my head. "Where would we even go this late?"

"There's that new nightclub that just opened."

"You mean Omega?"

She nods. "I heard the DJ plays the best music."

I sigh. "I don't exactly want to wear sunglasses in a nightclub."

"But it's already dark. No one would recognize us." She clasps her hands together. "Please? This will be our last chance to go out before MonsterMadness."

"I don't know…" I chew my lip. This feels like a bad idea. Going out without disguises is careless. What if we're seen?

Lena bats her eyelashes. "I'll sit on your face when we get back."

I cross my arms. "You really think you can bribe me with sex?"

"And pancakes?"

My mouth starts watering. "You would make pancakes?"

"As soon as I finish coming, I'll hop off and whip up some chocolate-chip pancakes."

Now, that's a tempting offer. All my worries about being recognized seem silly. It will be dark, and everyone will be too drunk to notice us anyway, right?

"There's just one problem…"

Lena tenses. "What's that?"

"I don't have anything to wear. I didn't come over with the intention of going dancing."

"That's an easy fix." She snaps her fingers.

"Oh really?"

"Yes. You can wear one of my graphic tees. I have a few that are loose on me, and one of them would make a perfect T-shirt dress for you. Just cinch it with a trendy belt."

"What about shoes?"

Lena waves me off. "Your black sneakers are fine. Stop making excuses."

It's foolish to even consider going out in public together without disguises, especially in such a crowded place, but I've been itching to do something other than sit inside or train at the gym. As much as I love staying in with Lena, going out sounds like a lot of fun and exactly what I need to blow off some steam.

I give my wings a determined flap. "Alright. Let's do it."

We do our makeup and hair, taking extra time to make ourselves look a little different, including Lena straightening her signature curls. After styling me in her favorite band shirt and belt, Lena changes into a slinky black dress and pumps that add an extra three inches to her already imposing height.

"You look hot." I practically drool at the way the dress hugs her hips.

"And so do you," she says, eyeing me up and down.

I twirl. "I do feel cute. Thank you for cutting holes for my wings. Though I feel kind of bad you ruined a shirt for me."

She steps forward and places her hands on my hips. "Totally worth it. I like seeing you in my clothes. Proves that you're *mine.*"

"There's that possessive streak." I chuckle.

"You knew what you were getting into when you decided to date a minotaur."

I roll my eyes with a smirk. "Whatever. Let's go."

We take a cab to avoid anyone looking too hard under the train's harsh lighting. The entire ride, we talk about what kind of songs we hope we hear and the possibilities on the cocktail menu.

Omega is housed in a red brick building with no indication that it's a swanky nightclub other than the small wooden sign next to the entrance and the line down the block.

"How long will this wait be?" I ask with a groan.

Lena winks. "Don't worry. I'm willing to bet they'll let a couple of EMW stars in."

"But we're supposed to be anonymous!"

"That's the best thing about clubs like this. Discretion." She pulls two pairs of sunglasses out of her purse. "Here. Wear these until we get through the door."

I nod, taking a pair. *Shit.* I hope this works.

Lena marches up to the orc bouncer, and I follow, trying to look just as confident. She whispers in his ear, and after giving me and her a long once-over, he nods and lets us through, much to the displeasure of those waiting in line.

Inside, Omega is all pink-and-blue neon with bright-purple floors and walls. The dance floor takes up the majority of the space while two large bars on either side span the walls. The DJ booth sits high, facing the crowd. A few small tables and chairs line the space between the dancers and the bar.

"Why don't you snag us a table?" Lena shouts over the house music. "I'll grab us drinks."

I give her a thumbs-up and begin making my way to the high-top table in the darkest corner. Perfect for us to enjoy our drinks in peace. After settling onto my stool, I survey the scene. Almost everyone is dancing, and there are even a few humans sprinkled into the mostly monstrous crowd. My taloned foot taps along to the beat. I'm eager to dance.

"Hey there, pretty thing," someone shouts in my ear.

A vampire stands next to me, dressed like he stepped out of a human Regency romance novel. His long blond hair is slicked back into a low ponytail, and his red eyes glow in the darkness.

"Can I help you?" I cock my head, offering him a forced grin, waiting to see if he recognizes me.

"My friend and I were just wondering what a beautiful thing like you was doing here all alone." He gestures to a handsome male kraken, dressed like a punk rocker, all black leather and piercings, contrasting against his green skin.

"I'm not alone," I respond.

He wiggles his brows. "Are you with an equally pretty friend?"

"It's true." I point behind him, where Lena is approaching with our drinks.

The vampire and the kraken look in her direction, grins spreading across their faces.

"She's lovely, too," the kraken says, flashing his sharp teeth.

Lena glares at the males as she hands me my drink. I take a sip, trying not to grimace at how heavy-handed the bartender was on the tequila. It tastes like shitty liquor with a squirt of bottled lime juice. Barf.

"Fancy a dance, love?" the kraken asks Lena.

The vampire shakes his head. "Let these lovely ladies finish their drinks first."

I frown. "What makes you think we want to dance with you?"

The vampire blinks rapidly, while the kraken narrows his eyes at me.

Lena steps between me and the two males, puffing her chest. "I advise you to get lost."

"Unbelievable," the kraken growls. "We're good-looking dudes. How dare you tell us to get lost."

"Sure." I shrug. "You are both handsome, but my girlfriend and I want to enjoy our drinks in peace."

The vampire blushes as he looks between me and Lena. "My apologies." He grabs his glaring companion by the biceps. "Let's get out of here."

"Whatever." The kraken flips us his middle finger. But the two males leave us alone, and that's all that matters.

"They didn't recognize you, did they?" Lena takes a sip of her drink, her face twisting in disgust as she swallows.

"Not that I'm aware of."

"Good." She swirls her glass. "I hated seeing that vampire schmoozing up to you."

I scoff. "You know I'm not into anyone but you. And especially not any males."

She shrugs. "This is *our* night. I don't feel like being polite to random horny dudes."

"Totally fair," I nod. "Let's finish these drinks and get out there. I'm ready to dance!"

Lena and I toss our heads back and guzzle the shitty drinks before heading to the dance floor, hand in hand. The music is so loud, we're forced to communicate via hand gestures and shouting in each other's ears. But it doesn't matter because the buzz from the cheap tequila and the pulse of the music makes everything else melt away. It's just her body against mine as we gyrate to the beat.

We dance until the lights flash for last call. We pull away from each other, gasping, skin flushed with heat and damp with sweat. I didn't even realize that much time had passed. Lena grabs my hand, leading me off the dance floor.

"We should get out of here and call a cab before it shuts down," Lena says in my ear.

I nod, and we slip out of the club and onto the street, where several cabs are lined up, waiting for passengers. We pick one, give the driver the address to Lena's apartment, and snuggle into each other.

I rub my hand up and down Lena's thigh, caressing her silky fur. She sighs and sinks lower into the seat. She looks so sexy right now. Her makeup is smeared, and her hair is a wild, curly mess, the heat and sweat destroying her silky, straight strands from earlier in the night. Top that off with the fact that one of the straps of her dress has slipped off her shoulder and she looks absolutely fuckable.

"Can you turn on some music?" I shout up to the cab driver.

Thank goodness he's human. Humans don't have the strongest of senses, and I need him to be completely unaware of what I'm about to do to Lena.

I press my mouth to Lena's ear. "Do you think you can be quiet?"

Chapter 19

Lena

I SHIVER AT IRIS'S QUESTION. Is she asking what I think she's asking? Her hand slides up my thigh and under my dress, her finger grazing the crotch of my silk panties.

Does she really intend to finger fuck me in the back of this cab?

"Are you sure about this?" I whisper, so the driver won't hear me over the cheesy pop music now blaring out of the car speakers.

"He's a human," Iris purrs in my ear. "He can't see or hear what I'm about to do to you."

Heat rushes to my pussy at her words. If fucking in the ring was risky, then we are playing with fire, considering the cab driver is only a few feet away from us. He may be human, with duller senses than most monsters, but we'll still have to be careful.

Iris sits back in her seat and looks out the window while she continues to stroke my heat through my thin underwear with her finger. We're really doing this? When she glides her finger against my clit through the silk, I suck in a breath.

I glance in the rearview to see if the driver noticed, but he's too busy swaying along to the love ballad playing on the radio, focused on the road. Closing my eyes, I relax into Iris's touch.

She chortles, just loud enough for me to hear, before using her fingers to push aside the fabric of my panties and give my clit skin-to-skin contact. Her touch is delicate, a whisper against my sensitive clit. Iris knows that I like to be teased to arousal, and she's taking her time.

She works my clit until my panties are soaked. I fight the urge to buck my hips, clenching my fists at my side to keep control.

Every time the cab driver glances in the rearview mirror to check the traffic, I tense. Does he know? And every time his gaze falls back on the road ahead, a thrill rushes through me. The cycle of anticipation and relief is intoxicating. I'm dizzy with excitement.

Iris ceases stroking my clit and dips two of her fingers into my entrance. My cunt clenches around her. She thrusts in and out of my throbbing, wet pussy in languid motions. When she curls her fingers to stimulate my sweet spot, I have to clamp my teeth into my lower lip to bite back a moan.

Out of the corner of my eye, I meet Iris's intense gaze. She holds mine for a few moments while she continues to fuck my pussy. With a smirk and a long dragging look up and down my body, she removes her fingers.

Using my slick, she rubs the sides of my clit with her index and middle finger. This is my absolute favorite way to be touched. It won't take long to send me over the edge if she keeps playing with me like this.

I can't help rolling my hips when she increases the pressure. Iris pauses, her lips turned down into a stern frown.

"You don't want to get us caught, do you?" she asks, leaning close enough for me to hear her but not the driver.

I shake my head.

"This greedy pussy of yours wouldn't like having to cut this short, would it?"

Once again, I shake my head.

"That's what I thought. Now, be good, quiet, and still. I don't want *anyone* else to know when you are coming. Just me. This wet cunt, your pleasure, is mine and mine alone."

I close my eyes, fighting back a whine. Her dirty talk almost makes me explode in climax. When she continues to rub my clit between her fingers, I nearly come unglued. But I dig my fingers into my palms, the bite of my nails in my flesh keeping me grounded.

But is it enough to keep me from crying out when I come? I'm not exactly quiet when I orgasm. Do I tell Iris to stop before it happens?

We can always continue this when we get back to the safety of my apartment.

The pleasure is too much. I can't think straight. All I know is that I need to be still and silent and I'll get what my body craves, what it needs.

Iris squeezes my clit between her fingers, and it sends me over the edge. My body clenches, and my cunt gushes as my orgasm crashes over me. I lose sight of Iris's beautiful smirking face as my eyes roll back in my head.

I finish coming with a gasp, totally spent. Iris slows her strokes on my clit, knowing I love to be eased from my peak. Just when I'm on the verge of overstimulation, she stops, but not before dipping her fingers into my pussy.

Iris brings her fingers, glistening with my cum in the streetlights, to her mouth. Tongue darting from between her lips, she licks at the moisture. My heart skips a beat and I want to check that the driver isn't seeing this, but I can't look away. She looks so fucking sexy right now.

With a smile, she inserts her fingers into her mouth, sucking off the remainder of my slick. I finally manage to tear my gaze away from her face and look at the driver. He appears bored, probably because the radio is now playing one of those obnoxious car dealership commercials.

I relax. We got away with it. And, fuck, if it wasn't one of the hottest things I've ever done. My panties are now uncomfortably wet. Thank the goddess we're almost at our destination.

Iris pats my thigh, a satisfied grin on her face. I can't wait to get her through the door of my apartment and let her know exactly how I feel about her fingering me in the back of a taxicab.

Chapter 20

Lena

THE LOUD TRILL OF MY phone ringing startles me from a deep sleep. Iris barely stirs, rolling over with a groan. My girlfriend may be an early riser, but she is a deep sleeper. I glance at the clock. It's six in the morning.

What the fuck? Who is calling this early? And on our day off before we start traveling for MonsterMadness. Anyone who would be calling us knows this. I reach for the receiver with a heavy sigh. This better be good.

"Hello?"

"Lena! Thank goodness you answered." It's June.

I sit up, her shaky tone of voice making me worry. "What's going on? Is Gianna o—?"

"I'm coming over," she cuts me off.

"What? June, what's happening?"

"I'll be there in a few. Is Iris with you?"

"Yes."

"Alright. See you soon."

"But, June…"

The dial tone responds instead of my friend.

Oh shit. Panic sits uneasy in my stomach, making me nauseous. I've never heard June sound like that before.

"Is everything okay?" Iris asks, her voice heavy with sleep.

"I don't think so. June is on her way over now."

Iris sits up in bed. “Did she say why?”

I shake my head. “She hung up before I could press her for details.”

She frowns as she looks at the clock. “But it’s barely past six in the morning.”

“I know. I’m trying not to freak out.” I clutch a pillow to my chest, hugging it tight against me as I take a few deep breaths.

“What do you think it could be?”

I unclench my jaw to answer her. “Not sure.”

“We leave for MonsterMadness tomorrow,” Iris whispers.

There’s a long silence. Whatever June is about to tell us can’t be good, and with MonsterMadness two days away, that does raise questions.

I lean forward and plant a kiss on her cheek. “One step at a time. Let’s get dressed first and wait for June.”

We dress and brew coffee in complete silence. As the machine gurgles, we stand in the kitchen, staring out the window.

It’s not long before there’s a knock on the door. I answer to reveal an out-of-breath June with a panicked look in her eye.

“Oh my goddess!” I usher her inside. “Are you okay?”

Iris hands her a glass of water, which June guzzles down.

“Thanks,” she says, handing the glass back.

“Did you run here?” Iris asks.

June nods. “I didn’t want to wait for a cab.”

Thankfully, June doesn’t live that far from me. I lead her to the kitchen island so she can sit on a bar stool. Iris and I stand around her, waiting for her to tell us what the fuck is going on.

My friend looks between me and Iris, her eyebrows pinched. “Where were you two last Saturday night?”

I try to get my days straight. It’s been such a whirlwind leading up to MonsterMadness that it’s hard to keep track of everything.

Iris frowns. “We went to that new club, Omega.”

June’s shoulders sag. “That’s what I was afraid you were going to say.”

She holds up a newspaper, clenched in her fist. How am I just now noticing that? June unfurls the paper and lays it on the counter, smoothing the pages.

Wrestling enemies seen cozying up at new nightclub. Is the EMW fake? reads the top headline in big, bold letters. Underneath, in full color, is a photo of me and Iris dancing together in the middle of a crowded dance floor.

I'm hit with a wave of nausea. The photo is crisp, and our faces are clearly visible. There's no denying that it's Helen Stronghorn and Athena Rainstorm.

Oh fuck! The two biggest rivals in the EMW seen together in a nightclub? Yeah. That doesn't look good.

Iris snatches up the paper, her eyes darting across the page. With a groan, she tosses it on the island. "I can't read this."

I pick up the paper and scan the article. Whoever took these pictures watched us dance together all night, then witnessed us leaving together. Thankfully, this onlooker didn't catch us kissing or doing anything that would indicate we are romantically involved. But still, Charlie is going to be pissed.

"I'm so sorry," June whispers. "I saw it on my morning jog, and I just didn't want you to find out from someone else."

"You did the right thing." I place a hand on her shoulder. "Better from you than from Cha—"

The phone ringing interrupts me. *Shit.* It's probably Gi calling to give me the bad news. I answer the phone without bothering to look at the caller ID. "Hello?"

"Lena?" a vaguely familiar voice responds.

"Yes?"

The caller clears their throat. "It's Zach, Mr. Palmer's assistant."

Oh. The blood drains from my face. "How can I help you?" I try to sound confident, but my question comes out in a squeak instead.

"Mr. Palmer requests your presence in his office. Immediately."

A chill shivers up my spine. He definitely saw the tabloid, and he's definitely not happy. What are we going to do? We broke character, and now it's plastered everywhere literally two days before the biggest wrestling event of the year.

"Hello?" the annoyed voice of Charlie's assistant interrupts my growing panic.

"Sorry." I cough. "Uh…yeah. I'll be there right away."

"One more thing. Is Miss Iris there with you?"

I debate lying. Iris and I were mandated to spend time together outside of work and away from the public eye, but in the current circumstances, it looks a little more damning right now, especially since we are trying to keep our romantic relationship a secret. But lying won't get us anywhere good. It never does.

"Yes," I croak. "She's here."

Iris clamps her lower lip in her teeth, her eyebrows furrowed.

The assistant sniffs. "Tell her to come along."

I swallow. "Understood."

"Goodbye."

And with a click, the assistant hangs up the phone, leaving me with the shrill sound of the dial tone.

"Who was that?" June asks, wringing her hands.

I glance at Iris, whose eyes shine on the verge of tears. "It was Charlie's assistant. Charlie wants to see me and Iris in his office… immediately."

The tears shimmering in Iris's eyes begin to fall down her cheeks. Reaching across the island, I take her hand in mine and offer her a comforting squeeze. I've never seen her cry before, and it breaks my heart. I want to hunt down whoever took our photo at the club and snap them in half.

But it wouldn't do us any good. The damage has been done, and it's time to face the consequences of our actions. Our stupid, stupid actions. The worst part is that going out that night was *my* idea. I'm the one who put us in this shitty position.

"What are you going to do?" June asks, chewing her bottom lip.

I shrug. "What can we do, other than see what Charlie says? Maybe he won't be so hard on us because of his relationship with my dad."

June nods. "He adores you. Plus, I hate to admit it, but he's pretty smart. He'll think of a way to spin this to save face."

Iris wipes her eyes. "You think?"

"Charlie has dealt with worse, I'm sure." I nod. "He's been in the business for decades."

Something about the statement feels like a lie. Sure, Charlie has probably had worse crises, but he's also temperamental. I have no idea what we're about to face.

"Alright." Iris gives me a watery smile. "Let's get this over with."

I kiss her on the cheek. "That's my girl."

June points to the tabloid. "Want me to take this with me?"

Iris grimaces. "Please. I never want to see that picture again."

"Care to explain what the *fuck* I'm looking at here?" Charlie tosses a fresh copy of the newspaper onto the desk.

He isn't even sitting in his usual laid-back manner. Instead, he's pacing the space behind his desk, hands clenched at his sides. His spray-tanned face is a deep red, and his blue eyes burn with rage.

I wince and glance at Iris. Her jaw twitches, but other than that, her expression is as cool as a winter day. I'm proud of her for getting her tears out before meeting with Charlie. He considers crying a sign of weakness, and he doesn't respect weak people. It's all bullshit, toxic masculinity.

Charlie slams a fist on his desk. "Are either of you going to fucking answer me?"

I choke back a gasp. I've never seen him this angry before, and I don't appreciate the way he's speaking to us. I've learned to let Charlie's outbursts roll off my shoulders, but he's never been so flat-out disrespectful and demeaning to me.

"Charlie," I begin, in what I hope is a calming voice. "I want to start off by saying that we're really sorry."

Somehow, Charlie's face flushes an even deeper red. "Your apology means jack shit to me. It doesn't change the fact that you two *ruined* the public image of the EMW. Now all the fans will definitely believe wrestling is fake. What the fuck were you thinking?"

I square my shoulders, not willing to let him intimidate me. "We were just trying to blow off some steam. We've been working so hard leading up to MonsterMadness."

"So, you go to a crowded nightclub *together*? What kind of fucked-up logic is that?" Charlie looks at me. "You know better, Lena. Why did you agree to go along with this?"

Iris stiffens. My face and neck grow hot. How dare he assume Iris was behind it?

"It was my idea," I say through clenched teeth, trying to hold back my growing rage.

Charlie's eyes narrow. "Get the fuck out of my office."

My jaw drops. "Are you serious?"

Iris stands, but Charlie focuses his glare on her. "Not you, Iris. You stay right there." He turns back to me. "Expect a call from my assistant later today. I'm still thinking about how much to fine you."

A fine? That's not too bad. I can handle that, and I'm sure Iris can, too. But why does he want to talk to her alone? My heart begins to race. This can't be good.

Charlie points to his door. "Out. Now. Each second you're in my face is another grand added to your fine."

I refuse to move. There's no way I'm leaving Iris alone with this asshole. Instead, I set my jaw and settle in my chair.

"Lena," Charlie says in a warning tone.

Iris places a hand on my arm. "Please," she whispers. "Just go."

I search her gaze. Is she putting on a brave face? Does she actually want me to leave? But her mouth is pressed into a firm line as she nods at me. Whatever is about to happen, she seems prepared to face it alone.

With a final glare at Charlie, I rise from my chair and exit the office, making sure to slam the door on my way out. Charlie's assistant shakes his head at me.

"What?" I snap.

His smile looks smug. "You're an idiot."

I stalk toward him, towering over his desk. "Do you mind running that by me again?"

He swallows, his air of superiority souring under my threatening stare. "I'll tell Charlie you're bullying me."

"Go ahead." I smirk. "Do you think he cares? I'm his biggest wrestler."

"But you also just jeopardized the entire company." He puffs out his chest. "You're on thin ice. You may sell out arenas, but there are other ways to punish you."

I cross my arms over my chest. "Oh yeah? Like what?"

That ugly confident smile is back on his face. "He may not touch his biggest superstar, but did you ever think about what he could do to those you care about?"

My blood runs cold. I shake my head to stop the room from spinning. Would Charlie really do something to Gianna and June? What about Iris? He doesn't know how deep our relationship goes, right?

"Ah!" the little fucker snickers. "I see I hit a nerve."

I want nothing more than to grab him by the shirt and punch him square in the face. But I don't. Instead, I stumble out of Charlie's office suite. I can't let my temper get the best of me right now. There's too much at stake.

Chapter 21

Iris

Charles Palmer stares at me with his icy gaze. I stare back, but I don't dare say anything. This is Mr. Palmer's show, not mine.

"Do you have any idea what you've done?" he asks in a low growl.

I nod. Going out with Lena was a mistake, one I should never have agreed to.

"Lena says it was her idea, but I know the truth." Charles finally sits in his chair, leaning across his desk, hands clasped in front of him. "You wormed your way into her good graces, put her guard down. I asked you two to get along, but that doesn't mean you get to go gallivanting around town."

"Understood, sir," I respond.

"Lena should have known better, but you are the one who should have said no. But you just can't resist being around her, can you? You grew up idolizing her father. Tell me, was leeching yourself onto Lena a ruse to get into the good graces of The Mighty Minos?"

I flinch, turning my head away from him. "No, sir."

"You know why I made you a heel, Iris?"

I shake my head.

"Because you're pathetic," he sneers. "You may have a lot of technical talent, but I knew you would never be champion material. The fans could never love someone like you. You just don't have the charisma to pull it off. But a villain who never tastes true victory? Now that was something the fans could sink their teeth into."

I stiffen, but I still keep my mouth shut.

"And I can smell the desperation on you." He licks his teeth. "You want to hold a championship title so bad. But that's not for Athena Rainstorm. It's for stars like Helen Stronghorn. All you're good for is being the Big Bad."

Mr. Palmer's confirmed my worst fear: that I will never win a championship. It stings. My nose tingles. *Oh shit.* I'm going to cry. *Get it together.* I inhale deeply, willing the prickling sensation in my eyes and nose to go away.

Charles snickers. "Is the big bad Athena Rainstorm about to cry?" He drums his fingers on his desk. "It must suck, realizing you're nothing more than fodder for the real stars. Which is why, after MonsterMadness, you're no longer employed with the EMW."

My feathers stand on end. "What?"

"You heard me. Iris, you're a pretty good wrestler, but you aren't worth much in star power. I don't need you on my roster. Not like Lena. And someone has to pay for your mistakes. You understand, don't you?"

"But, sir"—I lean forward, digging my nails into the armrests of the chair—"being a wrestler with EMW is my childhood dream. I love it here."

He snorts. "You should have thought of that before you went clubbing with your biggest rival."

This couldn't be happening. Fired? I clutch my chest as I struggle to breathe.

"I honestly would have kicked your sorry ass to the curb today, but with MonsterMadness in two days, I can't readjust the storyline." Charles shrugs. "Better make this last fight count. Now, get the fuck out of my office."

I rush to stumble out of his office, breezing past Zach and into the hallway with the elevators. Lena is waiting for me.

I fall into her arms and she pulls me close. "What happened? Are you okay?"

I look up at her, tears streaming down my face. "I'm fired."

"What do you mean you're fired?" Lena asks after a few heavy moments of silence.

"After MonsterMadness, they're writing me off and I'm no longer an employee with the EMW."

Lena shakes her head. "Wait. This isn't fair."

I shrug. What can be done?

"You mean to tell me that I'm just getting a fine and you're getting fired?" Lena asks, her voice becoming shrill. "But it was *my* idea!"

"Yeah," I snap. "But you are the EMW Realms Champion and the most beloved wrestler. He can't get rid of you. Meanwhile, I'm just a heel. Easily replaceable."

"But you're one of the best we have! It makes no sense."

"Someone has to take the fall for what we did."

I bury my face in my hands and sob. All I ever wanted was to be a wrestler in the EMW. There was never another option for me. Even when my parents and teachers begged me to think of any other career, I stood firm.

Now that dream is gone. I could try to go back to the independent circuit, but I can kiss my dreams of holding an EMW Realms Championship belt goodbye. And what about the family I've made here? This community of wrestlers means so much to me.

And what does that mean for me and Lena? I may be leaving the EMW, but I doubt that means we could suddenly be seen together. Mr. Palmer will likely tighten his hold on his wrestlers, making it even harder for them to live their own lives. All thanks to an impulsive and idiotic decision made by me and Lena.

Lena's large arms wrap around me, and I melt against her. "Everything is going to be okay," she murmurs against my hair.

I let out a sardonic guffaw. "How?"

"I'll threaten to quit if Charlie doesn't hire you back."

"Lena!" I pull out of her embrace so I can look her in the eye. "Don't throw away your career for me."

Her eyes narrow. "I can and I will."

"Shush!" I hiss, holding a finger to her lips. "Don't say those things. We all knew what we were getting into when we chose to work for Mr. Palmer. Please, Lena. Don't do anything stupid."

"I can't promise that."

"Please." I squeeze her arm. "For me."

Lena's ears twitch as she chews her bottom lip. "Fine," she finally says with a nod. "But this isn't over, by the way."

I give her a small smile. "We should get out of here before someone sees us."

"I don't care anymore." She pulls me against her.

"No." I push away and step back. "We caused a lot of damage. If Mr. Palmer sees us together, I worry what he'll do to you."

Lena sighs, her fists clenched at her sides. "I hate this."

"Me, too. But it's for the best."

"I don't see how."

"The EMW *needs* you, Lena. Our friends need you here. Who else is going to advocate for them?"

She flicks her tail in short, rapid bursts. "We should all quit."

I shake my head. "You think we should ask everyone to quit because you and I were idiots?"

Lena squares her shoulders. "Yes. I do."

"Don't be ridiculous." I shake my head.

"I'm not!" She crosses her arms over her chest. "I'm sure everyone on the roster would agree this is fucked up."

I set my mouth in a firm line. "No. We need to face the consequences of our actions."

Is it fair that Lena gets a fine while I get fired? No. But honestly, I was such a dumbass. I shouldn't have risked my career. Lena and I have been happy sneaking around, and maybe we could have eventually asked for a storyline where we become friends. But all of that is over now. I'm a disgrace.

"I quit!" Daphne declares, after I tell her and Pan I got fired over hot chocolate.

Pan nods. "Me, too."

"No!" My voice is shrill from panic. "I didn't tell you this so you would quit. Don't give up on your dreams because of my idiot mistake."

"Honestly, what you did is pretty stupid." Pan frowns.

"Hey!" Daphne scolds. "That's not fair."

Pan holds up a finger, signaling Daphne to quiet down. "But you know what's even more stupid? The fact that Charles Palmer wants us to never break character, as if the fans don't know."

Daphne and I blink at them.

They sigh. "Come on. What's the number one thing fans ask us? 'Is wrestling fake?' They aren't dumb."

"You know," Daphne says, rubbing her chin, "I think you're onto something. It always annoys me when they ask if it's fake because those bumps are real. But maybe that's part of the problem. Maybe the more we deny the true nature of the industry, the more fans will push back."

Pan nods. "Think about it. Wrestlers back in the human realm are allowed to break character, and their arenas are packed every performance."

My mouth tugs into a frown. "That's true. So, why does Mr. Palmer care so much about keeping us in character all the time?"

"I think it has to do with control," Pan suggests.

Daphne gasps. "Oh, my goddess, you're right. If he keeps up the illusion that wrestling is real, then not only does he control our in-ring persona but our personal lives as well."

The three of us are silent and I contemplate Charles Palmer and his nefarious way of handling the EMW. He fired me because he lost control of me. He probably would have fired Lena, too, if she wasn't such a big draw for fans. Plus, he has extra influence over her since he's so close to her father.

Daphne finally breaks the silence. "So, what do we do?"

I shrug. "There's nothing we can do."

Pan scoffs, flicking their tail. "Sure, there is."

"How could we possibly change the mind of the most powerful man in pro wrestling?" I ask.

"We organize," Pan answers with a wicked smile.

Daphne claps her hands. "Excellent idea, Pan! I bet June and Gianna will join as well."

"And I don't think it would be hard to convince others." Pan leans forward, excitement in their eyes. "We can't be the only ones who feel oppressed by Charles Palmer."

"Whoa!" I hold up my hands. "Wait."

My friends pause and look at me with small frowns on their faces.

"I don't want this." I shake my head. "I didn't want to start some sort of revolution based on *my* stupid actions. I just want to give the fight of my life at MonsterMadness and then pick up the pieces. Hopefully, you two and Lena still want to be a part of my life after. That's all that matters to me."

Daphne tilts her head. "I don't understand. You're just going to roll over. That's not the Iris I know and love."

I wince. She's not wrong. But she wasn't there for the things Mr. Palmer said to me.

I'm not worth whatever mutiny my friends want to plan. Especially when I was never destined to be anything more than a hated heel.

I've never felt less empowered, not even when I was busting my ass to save for wrestling school.

My friends leave my apartment pissed at me because I don't want to lead some sort of anti-Charles Palmer campaign. I just want to crawl into my bed and forget about the whole thing. Then I need to plan how to move forward with my life. Can I even go back to the independent circuit? I don't have the 'star power' to succeed. Will I just be another heel with no chance of a championship? The entire conversation with Mr. Palmer has taken the wind from my wings.

I have a decent nest egg from my EMW earnings. Going back to school is always an option. But what else would I even do? Nothing else has ever appealed to me.

The shrill ring of my phone startles me from my thoughts. Who else could be calling me? I've already received multiple phone calls from family members, including my mother, who started to cry when I told her I was fired. Honestly, I don't have the time to talk to whoever is calling me. I need to finish packing for Mountain City, so I can do MonsterMadness and say goodbye to the EMW forever.

But the phone continues to ring. Whoever is calling is not giving up. With a heavy sigh, I answer the phone.

"Hello?"

"Iris?" It's Lena.

A soft smile forms on my lips. Even though I only saw her a few hours ago, it's comforting to hear her voice. "Hey, Lena. What's up?"

"I was just calling to check on you."

"I'm doing as well as I can, I guess. Packing for tomorrow's trip."

"Me, too!" Lena's enthusiasm sounds forced, but I know she's just trying to remain positive for me.

"I'm almost done. Thank the goddess."

Lena clears her throat. "Are we okay?"

"Goddess!" I rush to say. "Of course we're okay."

Her relief is audible through the phone. "Okay. I know I'm being selfish for even asking, considering what's going on, but—"

I smile for the first time today. "I promise, it's fine. Charles Palmer may have taken my career from me, but I won't let him come between us."

"I'm happy to hear that." A long pause. "Do you want me to come over?"

"I wish." My wings sag. "But honestly, I need to be alone right now. Besides, we have a big travel day tomorrow."

"I understand." But Lena sounds dejected.

"But I'll see you soon, okay?" I smile for good measure.

Lena sighs. "I guess I better get going, then. Bye, Iris."

"Goodbye, Lena."

There's a click followed by the shrill dial tone.

And now I'm left alone again with my thoughts.

Chapter 22

Lena

I FLICK ON THE LIGHTS in my hotel room and breathe in the scent of fresh linen. It was a hard day traveling. The flights weren't long, but I've been stewing about Iris and the situation with Charlie since yesterday. I want to do something about it, but I don't know what.

Unfortunately, I need to call my dad. He left a message on my machine yesterday asking me to call him, probably about the damning photo in the paper, but I didn't have the energy to deal with him. I still don't want to, but if I don't, I'll have hell to pay.

I place my suitcase on the luggage rack, then flop onto the bed. Bracing myself, I reach for the phone and dial my father's number.

"Lena?" he answers.

"Hey, Dad." I force a smile. Even if he can't see me, he always says people can hear when you smile.

"I saw the paper and tried calling you yesterday. Is that really you in the photos?"

"It is," I answer with a sigh.

"What the hell is going on with you? You should know better." His voice is raised, irritation clear in his tone.

I bristle, clenching my fists. "Are you serious right now? You don't even bother to ask how I'm doing, just automatically berate me. Typical."

"What's that supposed to mean?"

"You never consider my feelings...ever." The words gush out of me like a geyser with too much built-up pressure. "Ever since I was a little girl. It's always about our legacy. And I'm sick and tired of always thinking about it. The pressure is too much. I just want to live my life the way I want to."

"You wanted this," he snaps. "You wanted to be a wrestler. I worked so hard during my time in the EMW so you could follow your dreams."

"But I'm more than just a wrestler!"

He lets out a defeated-sounding sigh. "All I wanted was for you to succeed."

"And all I ever wanted was a father who supports me," I respond in a near whisper.

The silence between us is deafening and heavy. Finally telling The Mighty Minos the truth is freeing. But did I just ruin the relationship with my father?

"Tell me what happened," he says softly, shattering the silence.

I blink. Wait. Did he finally listen to me for once?

"I just wanted a fun night with my friend before MonsterMadness," I confide, choosing to take a risk and trust him. "We've been working nonstop, and I just wanted to blow off steam and celebrate."

My dad snorts. "Why did you just lie to me?"

I huff. "What?"

"Are you really going to tell me that Iris is just a friend?"

"She is!"

"Come on, Lena. I know you better than that." I can almost see the quirk of his brow.

"Alright." My ears flatten, fearing what my father will say when I tell him the truth. "Iris is my girlfriend."

"Were you dating when I met her?"

"No."

"But you had feelings for her then, didn't you?"

"Yes," I admit. "I think I've had feelings for her for a long time."

A long silence. "Do you love her?"

My heart skips a beat. Memories of Iris and how she makes me feel when I'm with her flash through my mind, and butterflies swoop low in my stomach. She makes me feel safe, complete, and cherished.

"Yes," I blurt out. "I love her."

It's obvious. I didn't even have to think about it. I'm madly and deeply in love with Iris of the Harpy Clan.

"It must have been hard to keep your relationship a secret." To my surprise, his tone is sympathetic.

Tears pool in my eyes. "It was. So hard. I want nothing more than to shout how I feel about her from the rooftops."

"It's moments like these that reminds me why I always thought Charlie was a fool for wanting to lie to the fans."

I cough. "Wait. Seriously?"

My dad disagrees with a decision made by Charlie? I never thought I would see the day.

"It's stupid. I've been pushing him on it for years. Fans have been speculating on the validity of the sport for years. Not only that, but it would give us wrestlers more freedom."

"You never told me."

He sighs. "I didn't want you to get involved."

Thank the goddess I'm lying on the bed, or I might have fallen over.

"You there?" my dad asks after a few moments of quiet.

"Yeah." I shake my head. "Sorry. I just never thought you would disagree with Charlie on anything."

My dad laughs. "You would be surprised. I've been fighting with him for most of my career. And I'm calling to see if I'm going to have to fight him on his choice of disciplinary action regarding your outing."

I cringe. "He slapped me with a fine."

"Is it a lot?"

"Not really."

"While I hate the rule, a fine isn't the worst thing."

I bite my lip. "But he fired Iris."

"What?" my dad growls.

"Yeah." A tear rolls down my cheek. "It wasn't even her idea, but he fired her anyway."

"That's fucked up!"

I wipe at my tears. "I know. I want to do something, but Iris has begged me not to. I hate it."

My father hums into the phone, as if thinking. "She's a good partner, trying to look out for you like that."

"She really is." I smile. "I'm so lucky to have her."

"You know one thing I've always been proud of about you?"

I cock my head. "What's that?"

"Your ingenuity."

A lump rises in my throat. I've never heard my dad compliment me like this before. He usually praises my charisma, strength or work ethic. Never my intelligence.

"You really think so?"

I can hear the smile in his voice. "Yes. I trust you to figure something out."

"Thanks, Dad," I respond, a smile creeping up my cheeks.

"And one more thing. I'm sorry I haven't been there for you the way you needed me. I promise that I will be better, starting right now."

It's time for the main event. I pace behind the LED walls that separate me from the crowd of thousands. My normal preshow routine involves stretching and blasting music as loud as I can in my headphones, but my nerves have turned me into a walking wreck. I also haven't seen Iris yet today.

In fact, I haven't seen her since we left Charlie's office. We called each other last night but agreed not to see each other. The night before MonsterMadness should be reserved for rest and getting in the right mindset. This is the biggest match of our careers.

And the last for Iris.

The thought makes my blood boil. Goddess, I fucking hate Charlie.

"Hey," a soft voice greets me from behind.

I whirl around to face Iris. She looks stunning, dressed in a purple pleather bodysuit with a deep V-neck covered in fishnet to highlight her voluptuous breasts. Sexy little biker gloves adorn her hands, reminding me of how intimate they have been with my body. Her long hair is pulled back into a power pony, drawing attention to her stunning violet eyes. I want to wrap her in my arms and kiss her, but I hold back.

"Hey." I smile.

Iris eyes me from horns to hooves, and my heart flutters. "You look amazing," she tells me.

I look down at my ring attire. My usual crop top and chaps of sky blue and silver are now white and rose gold.

"Thank you. You look incredible yourself."

Her blush is adorable. "Thanks."

I clear my throat when a ghoul production assistant walks by, eyeing us. I get the distinct impression Charlie asked them to keep tabs on us.

"Are you ready?" I ask.

She nods once, her mouth set in a line. "As ready as I'll ever be."

I open my mouth to say something, anything, to let her know that it's all going to be okay, but the production assistant approaches us.

"You're up," she says, tapping her clipboard with a pen.

"Alright." But I don't take my eyes off Iris.

My music queues.

It's time.

Chapter 23

Iris

THE CROWD JEERS AS I step through the ropes, joining Lena in the ring. She glares at me, cracking her knuckles. I smirk and blow her a kiss, taunting her for the audience. Her eyes widen, but she quickly course-corrects and deepens her frown. I hold back a giggle, pleased I made her break character, even if I'm the only one who noticed. This is the last time I will be in the ring, so I might as well have fun, even if I can't stand the boos echoing throughout the arena.

Lena holds up the EMW Realms Championship belt over her head. Her fans go nuts, chanting, "Mother! Mother! Mother!"

Ivy, the ring announcer, introduces the match, but I tune them out. This is about putting on the best match of my career. Thank the goddess we ran through the big moves so much. I can't wait to feel it all flow together.

After Lena passes her belt to the official, the bell rings three times and Lena rushes me. I dodge at the last second by dropping to my back and rolling out of the way. She attempts to stomp me, but I dive, barely avoiding her hoof.

Jumping to my feet, I beckon Lena. "Come get me!"

She circles me with slow, cautious steps. It's my turn to make a move. I kick high, aiming a talon at her face. It connects, and the crowd boos. Lena grabs her nose and pretends to check for blood. I don't hesitate and kick again.

This time she grabs my foot. With a smirk, she twists, sending me flipping through the air before I crash onto the mat. I howl to sell the bump, and Lena pumps her fists in the air, whipping the crowd into a frenzy.

Before I can recover, Lena drops to pin me. The human official slams their hand on the ground to count down.

"One!" they shout. "Two!"

But I kick out.

The match continues. Lena and I exchange blows, taking turns having the upper hand and unsuccessfully pinning each other. We make improv calls and execute the big moves with perfection. The crowd is into the match, chanting, "This is awesome!"

The official keeps time, occasionally telling us how long we've been wrestling. When we reach the thirty-minute mark, we're exhausted, but the show isn't over yet. I still have to suplex Lena off the top rope before her big finisher.

Lena knocks me to the mat with a kick to the midsection. I lay there, clutching my stomach as she climbs the ropes. Once she reaches the top rope, she spreads her arms wide. The audience cheers. They expect her to leap through the air before slamming into me.

But I don't let it happen. I leap to my feet and rush up the ropes to punch her in the face. Lena reels back, acting dizzy and going limp. I position myself for the suplex, just like we practiced, carefully balancing myself so we don't fall prematurely.

The crowd shrieks. They know what's about to happen. With a bounce, Lena and I fling ourselves off the rope. I lean back, pulling her over my head and flipping her upside down so we both land on our backs at the same time with a loud smack.

Lena howls in pain while I sit up, wincing and rubbing my lower back. I take a few moments to recover and increase the tension in the arena. The fans are on their feet. Will Athena Rainstorm pin the great Helen Stronghorn? How will the Mother recover from this?

I crawl toward Lena. When I reach her, I spread her legs and press my hips against her. The official drops to their knees and begins the count. This is the big moment. Lena will kick out, impressing the fans before completing her big finisher and winning the match.

"One!" the crowd roars. "Two!"

I wait for the kick out. What is taking her so long? The official hesitates, not daring to slam their hand into the ring for a third time. They know Lena is supposed to win.

Is she okay? I crane my neck to look at her. She's smiling, her eyes bright and mischievous.

What is she doing?

The official can't hold back any longer. Not without ruining the show.

"Three!"

The bell rings three times. The fans scream, a cacophony of boos and cheers. Their beloved hero just lost to the most hated heel in the Elite Monster Wrestling, winning the Realms Championship.

But I can't move. Did I really just win? This must be a dream. The official helps me to my taloned feet, but I'm in a daze. I should be celebrating and staying in character, but I'm too stunned to do anything other than gape at Lena.

"And your winner and new Elite Monster Wrestling Realms Champion, Athena Rainstorm!" Ivy croons into the microphone.

The official grabs my hand and pulls my arm into the air. My music begins to play. This is really happening. I won the championship I've dreamed of winning since I was a little girl.

Suddenly, the belt is in my hands. I stare down at it in awe. It's gleaming gold and gemstones glint under the lights of the arena. It's the most beautiful thing I've ever seen.

After Lena, of course.

She's now sitting up, grinning at me like this is the best day of her life. The realization hits me like a truck: Lena did this for me. She just made my dream come true when I was told it would never happen.

I drop to my knees so I can look her in the eye. "Are you sure?"

She nods. "I've never been surer of anything in my life."

My heart soars. "Thank you."

"I love you, Iris."

A large smile spreads across my face. I'm finally holding the EMW Realms Championship in my hands, but all that matters to me is Lena. She's my real dream come true, my real chance at true happiness.

I lay the belt on the mat and lean forward until we're only a few inches apart. "I love you too."

And then I grab Lena's face and pull her in for a kiss for all the world to see.

Chapter 24

Virginia Lavender

"Oh, my goddess!" I leap from my seat as Athena Rainstorm pulls Helen Stronghorn to her, their mouths crashing together. "Are they—"

"They are!" Nikolas finishes my sentence, mouth agape.

The audience's cheers are ear-piercing. I've never heard such a loud crowd before. But nothing like this has ever happened at an EMW show. This is new territory, and I'm not sure how to respond. I doubt Nikolas knows how either.

"There you have it, beloved viewers," Nikolas finally manages to say. "Athena Rainstorm is *kissing* Helen Stronghorn, and the former champion is kissing her back."

When the couple finally breaks from their kiss, they embrace one another. Tears flow down Athena's cheeks, and Helen wipes them away. It's obvious the two know each other intimately.

"This is awesome!" the crowd chants.

My smile is genuine. "The live audience here tonight in Mountain City is loving this."

Athena and Helen look around, as if unsure that they are hearing the fans correctly. The chant becomes even louder. After a few moments, they both break out in wide smiles. Helen kisses Athena on the cheek and stands. She picks up the cast aside belt and holds out her hand to Athena. Once Athena is standing, Helen passes the belt to the new champion with a proud grin.

The two former rivals look around the arena, waving to the roaring crowd. Helen whispers something in Athena's ear. Athena nods. The two step out of the ring and begin to walk hand-in-hand toward the LED screens that will lead them out of the arena. Fans reach over the barricades, desperate to touch the wrestlers, but Athena and Helen only have eyes for each other.

"They are cute together, aren't they?" I nudge my fellow commentator.

Nikolas snaps his beak. "They are. Who would have thought Athena Rainstorm and Helen Stronghorn are actually an item?"

"This just proves anything can happen at MonsterMadness."

Chapter 25

Lena

When Iris and I step behind the LED screens, a mob of production assistants and writers rushes us.

"What have you done?"

"Why did you do that?"

"Way to go!"

But Iris and I can't take our eyes off each other. And it's a huge weight off my shoulders to let the whole world know that we're together. Consequences be damned.

"Excuse me." Zach pushes his way through the crowd, a smug smile on his face. "Mr. Palmer needs to see you two in his office. Immediately."

I square my shoulders and grip Iris's hand tighter. "Lead the way."

His grin falters. "Right this way."

We follow the assistant, giggling the whole time. I don't care what Charlie has to say. In fact, I'm going to give the bastard a piece of my mind. Iris may not be happy that I'm quitting, but I can't bring myself to continue working for someone who abuses us like this.

The assistant opens the door to the temporary office to reveal a very pissed-off Charlie pacing the room. His face is redder than a tomato, and his hair and mustache look like he's been tugging on them. Gone is the carefully groomed image he puts out into the world, replaced by a man who looks on the verge of tears.

"What the fuck was that?" he screams. He turns to Iris. "Was this *your* stupid idea? Is this your way of getting back at me for firing you?"

I step between him and Iris. "No, Charlie. This was *my* idea. Iris had no clue I was going to do that."

His eyes narrow. "You're telling me that *you* fucked over this company?"

"No. I fucked over *you.*" I jab a finger in his chest.

"I am this company!" Charlie shrieks, spittle flying from his lips.

The sound of the door opening startles me.

"Are you sure about that?" my dad asks.

"Victor?" Charlie growls. "Don't you know how to fucking knock? Also, I'm busy here with your dumbass daughter."

Zach stumbles through the doorway. "I'm sorry, sir. I tried to stop them."

"Them?" Charlie's eyes bulge.

Gianna, June, Pan, and Daphne file into Charlie's office with determined looks on their faces.

"There are more of us outside," Pan says with a smug smile.

Gianna lets out a condescending snicker. "Actually, it's the whole roster."

"What the fuck is going on?" Charlie's gaze darts between our friends and my father.

Pan crosses their arms over their chest. "We heard what you did to Iris. And, quite frankly, we think it's bullshit."

Charlie's face twists into a sneer. "I don't give a shit what you think!"

My dad tilts his head. "You might want to."

"Oh yeah?" Charlie turns to my father, fists clenched. "And why is that?"

"Because we quit," June states, hands on her hips.

Wait.

What the fuck is happening?

Charlie throws back his head in a laugh. "Is this some kind of sick joke?"

Daphne steps forward. "We mean it. Your entire roster is quitting."

Charlie's face falters. "You can't be serious."

"We are!" someone shouts from the hallway, followed by a chorus of agreements.

I finally look at Iris. Lips parted and eyes wide, she appears to be in shock.

"Are you okay?" I ask, giving her hand a squeeze.

She blinks a few times. "Is this really happening? Because of me? Did you know about this?"

I nod. "It looks like it, and no, I didn't know this was going to happen."

"But—"

"Hush," I whisper, kissing her cheek. "I believe this was a long time coming."

I turn my attention back to the spectacle unfolding before us.

Charlie throws his hands up in the air. "Fine! I'll hire Iris back on."

Pan shakes their head. "That's not good enough."

"What?" Charlie swallows. "What will it take to keep you from quitting?"

Pan smiles. It looks sweet and innocent, but I know better. "We won't quit the EMW under one condition."

Charlie lets out a sigh of relief. "Whatever you want."

Pan's smile turns sharp. "You quit."

The room spins and I grasp onto Iris to keep from falling over.

"I *own* this company." Charlie sputters. "You really think I'm going to quit?"

My father nods. "Yes, Charlie. You're going to take a very generous buyout and quit. How are you going to run a company with no wrestlers? And I doubt anyone on the indie circuit will want to work for you when they hear your entire roster mass quit."

Charlie pales. "You wouldn't really do this to me, would you?"

Gianna nods. "We would."

"You know this company is going to collapse without my expertise. Who else is going to run this company and make a profit?"

My father grins. "Me."

My father is going to run the EMW? But it makes sense. He knows the industry better than anyone.

Charlie snorts. "Seriously?"

"You don't think I'm capable?" My father cocks his head. "I learned so much from you during my tenure."

"Fuck," Charlie whispers, tugging on his mustache.

"But don't worry, old friend. I'm going to offer you a fair price to buy out the company. Expect an offer sometime next week."

Charlie's glare bounces around the room before finally landing on Iris. "This is all your fault," he seethes.

I growl and step toward him with clenched fists, prepared to show him *exactly* how I feel about him.

"Actually," my dad quips, "it's yours. If you had been reasonable, we wouldn't be having this conversation."

"Fuck all of you," Charlie snaps.

My father crosses his arms over his chest. "I take it you accept our terms?"

Charlie stomps toward the exit, turning around right before he steps through the doorway. "You better offer me a good deal."

Once Charlie's heavy footsteps are finally out of earshot, my father's face breaks out into a large grin. "Congratulations everyone. We did it!"

The small crowd assembled both inside and outside of the office erupts in cheers. I look at Iris. Tears are streaming down her cheeks which are pulled into a large smile. With a joyous laugh, I swoop her into my arms in a tight embrace. She sighs and flaps her wings to capture my mouth with hers. My heart soars as I melt into her kiss.

The small crowd coos, startling me and Iris apart.

"You two are so cute!" June says with a dreamy smile.

My father claps a hand on my shoulder. "I'm glad you found someone who makes you happy."

I brush a stand of Iris's hair that's fallen from her ponytail off her face. "I've never been happier."

Iris grins at me, then turns to our fellow wrestlers. "Thank you. I cannot even begin to express how much it means to me that you all came to my defense."

Pan and Daphne step forward and wrap Iris in a group hug, while everyone chatters a chorus of various sentiments, everything from "glad to do it" to "finally out from under that asshole." The general consensus is satisfaction.

My dad claps his hands to get everyone's attention. "My first order of business will be to get rid of this being in character all the time business if you don't want to be. I was sick of pretending to hate my friends outside of the ring and always being in character. I'm sure everyone here is, too."

We erupt in more cheers and applause. Finally, we're free.

Chapter 26

Iris

Fans and reporters swarm Lena and me as we leave the arena, bombarding us with questions. We refuse to comment, but we openly hold hands. Let them speculate. Victor wants to hold a press conference tomorrow when we are back in Metroville, where all their questions will be answered. For now, we just want to celebrate.

When we stumble into my hotel room, I immediately shimmy out of my clothes. "Join me in the shower?"

We didn't shower in the locker room after our match because we couldn't wait to be alone. And now I just want her by my side.

Lena grins as she pulls her crop top over her head. "I thought you would never ask."

I giggle and scurry to the bathroom to start the shower. By the time Lena joins me, the water is steaming.

Lena steps into the hot water and lets out a long sigh. "Get in here, champ." She beckons me with a finger.

"Champ?" I laugh.

"Correct me if I'm wrong, but aren't you the EMW Realms Champion now?"

I can only imagine how goofy I look right now with my giant smile. "I am."

"So, get in here." She laughs. "Time to get you squeaky clean."

Thankfully, the shower is large enough to accommodate both of us and my wings. The hot water feels amazing on my sore and bruised body. I let out a loud groan. Nothing feels better than a shower after a match.

Lena grabs a washcloth and a bar of soap, lathering the soap until bubbles form. With a wicked grin, she motions for me to turn around. Heat rushes to my pussy from the way she looks at me. I oblige and show her my back.

"Are you ready, my champion?" Lena asks, her voice husky.

I suck in a breath. Fuck. Being called 'my champion' is pretty hot. I could get used to this.

"I am." I adjust my wings to give her better access to my back.

The washcloth drags against my skin deliciously. Lena scrubs at my back in slow circles with one hand while the other uses the slick lather to massage my muscles. I moan and grip the bar of the shower door to keep my knees from buckling in pleasure.

Lena wraps her arm around my waist. "I got you," she murmurs into my ear.

I shiver despite the heat of the water, and my cunt clenches. If I reached between my legs, I'm positive I would already be wet enough to fuck.

While the hand with the washcloth continues washing my back, the one around my waist slides to my breasts. With her hand still slick with soap, Lena begins to massage one of my breasts. When her thumb swipes over my nipple, I inhale through my teeth and press my ass against her.

She chuckles. "What do you want?"

"You know what I want." I pant.

"I want to hear you say it."

"I want you to fuck me." I look over my shoulder at her with a pout.

She tuts. "So needy. You're not even clean yet."

"Shut up and fuck me already," I groan, arching my back.

"Yes, my champion," she purrs as she pinches my nipple.

I buck my hips, but Lena stills me with a firm grip, abandoning the washcloth. The hand that was previously scrubbing my back slides up my side to cup my other breast. Her thumbs circle my nipples.

"Lena!" I gasp, pressing my back against her, aching for more.

She nips my ear and trails down my stomach before dipping a finger into my soaked entrance. I hiss as she glides a second finger into my cunt. With achingly slow thrusts, Lena coats her fingers with my slick.

"I can't believe you're so wet for me already. I barely even touched you," she murmurs against my ear.

I gasp when Lena slips her fingers out of my pussy.

"Don't worry," she assures me. "I wouldn't deny my champion."

A whine releases from my throat when Lena barely grazes my clit, sending a jolt of pleasure through my body. Fuck. She knows exactly how to drive me wild. I moan when she increases the pressure, alternating between circling my clit with her index finger and lightly tapping it. The change in sensation keeps me from spilling over the edge. It's sweet torture.

Her hand still playing with my nipple slides down my back, grazing the sensitive base of my wings, which sends a shiver up my spine. Right before it becomes too much, Lena glides a hand down my ass and gives it a hard squeeze.

"Hands on the wall," Lena says.

I lean forward and place my hands on the shower tiles. While still rubbing my clit and gripping my ass, she uses her knee to part my thighs. My cunt is exposed and aching for her touch. I open my mouth to beg when she reaches between my thighs from behind and thrusts two fingers inside my dripping cunt.

"Oh fuck!" I moan, my talons digging into the shower floor.

Something wet and heavy lashes against my nipple. I look down to see that she's caressing my breasts with the soaked tip of her tail. The damp bristles of her tail tuft are rough and slippery on my hard peaks.

Lena starts thrusting her fingers in and out of my pussy while the fingers on my clit match the brutal pace. The sound of my sopping wet cunt getting fucked can be heard even over the roar of the shower.

I throw my head back. "Lena!"

"Is this enough for my champion to come?"

"Yes!" My answer is strangled as she slips a third finger inside me.

"It was so hot the way you pinned me in the ring." Lena fucks me to the base of her knuckles, the stretch of her three fingers delightful.

"If we hadn't been on live TV in front of thousands of fans, I would have fucked you right then and there."

Between the rough texture of her tail on my nipples, the soft pad of her finger on my clit, and the brutal pace of her fingers in my cunt, I can't keep my eyes open. I lose myself to the euphoria of having Lena's hands on me, working me to a frenzy.

"Oh, goddess," I whine and buck my hips, matching her thrusts.

Lena growls. "It's just me and you in here, my champion. I want you screaming *my* name."

Fuck. Possessive Lena is hot.

She curls her fingers in my cunt, stimulating my G-spot. "I don't hear my name."

"Lena!" I scream, stars exploding behind my eyes. If there is anyone in the room next to us, they definitely hear me.

"Again."

I sob. "Lena!"

My orgasm crashes into me, intense and overwhelming. Everything else fades to black other than Lena and her ministrations on the sensitive parts of my thoroughly fucked body.

"Lena! Lena! Lena!" I chant her name like a prayer.

"That's it. Come for me, my champion," she whispers, gentle and reassuring, but she doesn't ease her onslaught.

With a final gasp, I crash from my peak. Lena catches me before I slip on the tile.

"I got you. I got you." Lena promises.

I'm exhausted. The physical exertion of the match, the thrill of winning, the excitement of defeating Charles, and, finally, the crash of my orgasm has caught up to me. I groan when the washcloth returns to scrubbing at my skin.

"Let's finish washing you up. Then I'll get you to bed," Lena says, her voice now soft and soothing.

I barely notice her turning off the water and stepping out of the shower to wrap a fluffy towel around me. Lena scoops an arm under my legs and lifts me as if I'm a blushing bride, careful not to crush my wings. I wrap my arms around her neck and allow her to carry me to the soft, plush bed.

She lowers me to the mattress. "Do you need anything else, my love?"

"A kiss?" I mutter, my eyes already closed.

"I can do that." Her lips graze gently against mine. "I'm going to finish my shower and then join you. How does that sound?"

I hum in agreement.

"I love you, Iris."

"I love you, Lena."

And that's the last thing I remember before drifting off.

Chapter 27

Lena

"Are you ready for this?" I ask, nudging Iris with my elbow.

She nods. "I'm a little nervous. What if they still hate me?"

I take her hand in mine. "They won't. Haven't you seen the papers?"

Since MonsterMadness, the world of pro wrestling has been turned upside down. My father kept his promise and announced to the masses that the EMW was scripted but reminded everyone of our very real athleticism and hard work. Fans took it really well. In fact, attendance at shows has been up. It turns out that being honest with your audience goes a long way.

Iris and I held a press conference and officially made our relationship public. The gathered journalists met our announcement with cheers, applause, and words of support.

Our MonsterMadness EMW championship match smashed the record for the highest-rated event by fans. My father gave us and our shocking kiss all the credit.

He had the brilliant idea to make us a tag team, Tough Love. Tonight is our first match, and we're gearing up for our prematch promo. Iris is extremely nervous. Despite all the positive feedback, she's afraid the fans won't see past her former persona as a hated heel.

Hazel, who is interviewing us tonight, fluffs her hair. "I'm ready whenever you two are."

Iris looks at me and motions toward her outfit. "Do I look okay?"

We kept our signature outfits but recolored them in various shades of pink. Honestly, the colors look perfect against Iris's light gray skin.

I squeeze her hand. "You look beautiful."

She smiles and looks at Hazel. "I'm ready."

Hazel clears her throat and motions for the wolven camera operator to get into position. The wolven counts down and then we're live. When we appear on the arena's screens, the cheers of the crowd echo all the way to the back halls.

"I'm here with Athena Rainstorm and Helen Stronghorn, also known as Tough Love," Hazel begins. "This is your first match together as a tag team. How do you feel as you prepare to go up against The Twins?"

The Twins, a pair of ghouls who aren't actually related, have been practicing with us. They are excellent wrestlers who work well together and gave Iris and me a lot of pointers on how to communicate in the ring. I'm almost a little sad they are scripted to lose to us, but the best thing about the new leadership under my father is that we have a chance to shift between different roles. The Twins will get their chance to be winners one day.

"I've never felt more ready," Iris says with a flap of her wings.

I nod. "The Twins don't know what's coming."

Hazel smiles. "How have you two prepared for this match?"

Iris answers. "We've spent all our training time in the ring practicing double-team maneuvers on top of our regular strength and cardio training."

"Do you think your romantic chemistry will help or hinder your match?" Hazel asks.

I hold up our clasped hands. "Help, for sure. We work so well together and understand one another's needs. The Twins may have a few years of tag team experience on us, but they don't know the bond of two wrestlers in love. Plus, we both have held the EMW Realms Championship. Can The Twins say they've done that?"

Hazel's eyes flash. "Helen, how does it feel to date the EMW Champion? Is there any jealousy considering she stole the title from you?"

"None." I kiss Iris on the cheek. "I had a good run as the champion, but if I was going to lose it to anyone, I'm happy to lose to the best. And it's clear to me and everyone else on the roster that Athena is the best. I've never been more proud."

Hazel looks at Iris. "And how do you feel about those sweet words from Lena?"

Iris grins, looking at me instead of Hazel as she answers. "I have never felt more loved in my life."

Hazel coos. "You two are so cute."

I snicker. "Yeah but we're far from cute in the ring. The Twins are in for a double dose of Tough Love."

Hazel smirks and turns to the camera. "There you have it, folks. Tough Love feels confident going into tonight's match against The Twins."

The crowd roars. The cheers are muffled from backstage, but that just means it will be thunderous when we walk into the arena.

Hazel lowers the mic, indicating the live feed has wrapped up. "Excellent interview. We'll chat again after the match." She waves as she saunters down the hall to find her next interview. "Good luck out there."

I glance at Iris, who is nibbling her bottom lip.

"You hear them, don't you?" I murmur in her ear. "They're cheering for *us.*"

"They're cheering for *you,*" she responds, "not me."

"We shall see."

A human production assistant with a clipboard rushes us. "Time to go."

Iris and I follow them to the arena entrance. Our music cues, a romantic yet upbeat melody. Iris sucks in a deep breath, and we step out from behind the LED screens. The cheers are deafening. I spare a side glance at Iris to check on her, but she's in character, swaying her hips to the music.

We slap hands with fans reaching over the barricade. They scream for both Helen Stronghorn and Athena Rainstorm. Iris's stage grin becomes a genuine one as she takes in several signs in the audience displaying both our names.

As we climb into the ring, we wave to the frenzied crowd. Once inside, we climb to the top turnbuckle together and kiss.

Kissing Iris never gets old, and it's especially thrilling and special now that we no longer have to hide our relationship. Throwing my MonsterMadness match was the best decision I ever made.

"True Love always wins!" the audience chants. "True Love always wins!"

Tears shimmer in Iris's eyes. The smile on her face is even bigger than when she won the EMW Realms Championship.

They love us. They love *her.*

Commercial Break

Tough Love Action Figures

ATHENA RAINSTORM AND HELEN STRONGHORN burst through a wall painted with the Elite Monster Wrestling logo.

"Are you ready to fight?" Helen asks, flexing her biceps.

Iris spreads her wings. "Are you ready for some Tough Love?"

The scene cuts to two toy figurines of Athena Rainstorm and Helen Stronghorn sporting the Tag Team Championship belts around their waists.

"If you answered yes," Helen's voice announces off-screen, "get excited for our new and exclusive action figures."

Two children—one a werecat and the other a dragon—each hold a figure, large smiles on their faces.

"The strongest tag team around, Tough Love is now sold together," Iris's voice announces over footage of the children moving the figures to a toy-sized ring. "Now create your dream roster in one purchase, featuring our updated tag team outfits."

"Who will *you* have us fight?" Helen asks and the werecat child collides their Helen action figure with an action figure of one of the ghouls from The Twins.

"Smash, slam, and fight your way to victory with the Tough Love action figure set," Athena's voice says as the dragon child zooms their Athena figure through the air.

The scene cuts back to Athena and Helen, each holding an action figure of themselves.

Athena holds out her figure. "The Tough Love set can be found anywhere toys are sold. Ring and ring accessories sold separately."

"I dare you challenge us!" Helen flexes her pecs.

Athena flaps her wings. "Make your wrestling dreams a reality."

The image of the two wrestlers standing together with their action figures fades to black.

Epilogue

Iris

Almost One Year Later

With a grunt, Lena deposits the cardboard box onto the living room floor. It's the last item from my apartment. I'm officially moved into Lena's condo.

"Thank you." I stand on my toes to kiss her cheek.

"I'm just happy you're here now."

I release a dreamy sigh. "Me, too. Now we can finally celebrate."

Lena grins. "What are we celebrating? Moving in together or winning the Tag Team Championship?"

I shrug. "Why not both?"

Since debuting as a tag team, Lena and I have become fan favorites. We finally won the tag team championship last week. It's a dream come true for me to be cheered instead of booed. Even when I wrestle solo to defend the EMW Realms Championship Title, I get the face treatment from the crowd.

Lena laughs. "We might as well celebrate both, considering MonsterMadness is in two weeks. When will we have time to cut loose until then? Especially since you have two matches to train for."

"Exactly."

Lena and I are slated to remain the Tag Team Champions, but I'll be passing the EMW Realms Championship to Daphne. I couldn't be more excited for her. She's earned it.

"Should we invite everyone over?" Lena asks as she pushes the box to the corner with all my other boxes from the move.

"But I still have to unpack."

She shrugs. "Who cares? That's all part of a housewarming party experience."

"Is it really a housewarming party if you've already lived here for a few years?"

"But *you* haven't." Lena nuzzles my nose with her snout.

I sigh. "Fine. We'll invite everyone over." It's hard to deny Lena anything.

"Great! I'll call them, and I have plenty of food in the pantry to whip up some yummy snacks for everyone."

"Can you make mini pizzas?" I bat my eyelashes at her.

She laughs. "Of course." Her ears perk. "But can we do something first?"

"What's that?"

"Can we finally hang our paintings?"

"Of course." I grin.

Our paintings from last year sat in my closet all this time, unhung. We kept talking about putting them up but kept delaying, playfully bickering about whose place to display them at. We always joked the perfect solution was to live together.

Now that I'm finally moved in, we have no excuse.

Lena digs through the corner of all my stuff and pulls out our landscape paintings. "Where do you think they should go?"

I look around the condo, my gaze finally falling on a blank area above the sofa. "What about there?" I point.

"Perfect! The box of hanging tools is in the laundry room."

When I return with the nails, hammer, ruler, and level, Lena has already picked the spot on the wall where she wants the paintings. I assist, handing her whatever tools she needs. She hums to herself as she meticulously measures everything.

"There!" Lena steps back, hands on her hips. "How does that look?"

The paintings are hung straight and even and look fantastic next to each other.

"You did great." I rest my head on her shoulder.

She kisses the top of my head. "We should paint more. This whole wall should be our art."

I hum. "Sounds perfect."

"Just like you."

"I love you, Lena," I say, turning my head so I can look into her eyes.

"And I love you, Iris."

Lena wraps her arms around me and lifts me. My mouth meets hers in a soft kiss. But what starts as tender and loving escalates to something more heated when I tease my tongue over her bottom lip. Before I know it, our tongues intertwine and my hands are tangled in her curls. Her hands grip my ass.

"Fuck!" She pants, breaking the kiss. "If we're going to have our friends over, I should start on the food."

"No one is on their way right now. We have some time," I mutter as I pepper her jaw with kisses.

"So greedy," Lena teases but begins walking me toward the bedroom.

"But what better way to welcome me home than with an orgasm or two?"

"Well, when you put it that way…"

I sigh with happiness. Nothing in the realms compares to being in love with Lena. Not even winning gold.

Acknowledgements

Wow! Another round of acknowledgements, and this one is going to be a doozie because so much went into writing *Pinned by Love*.

I can't write a book without my lovely beta readers. To Iris, for always coaching me through how to better. To Deanna and Lizzy, for giving such important feedback while also giving me the confidence to keep going. To Lydia, for confirming that I was on the right path with the wrestling aspects. And, finally, to Lexie for loving the Commercial Breaks as much as I do.

Thank you to Rouge for bringing Iris and Lena to life! You did amazing, and I look at their character ref sheets daily. Also, thank you for asking to add makeup to their costumes. What a brilliant move!

To Astrid. Thank you for believing in this story and taking a chance on it. I was worried it was going to be too weird, but I was thrilled to hear you loved it and wanted it to be a part of Ylva Publishing.

Hey, Sarah! Are you tired of having to correct me on the same old stuff yet? Haha! But seriously, I'm sorry I haven't learned to tag internal dialogue on my own yet. Maybe next time. Thank you for being such a patient editor who takes the time to teach me. It means a lot to have you on my team.

Where would this story be without Becky Lynch? Yes, I'm talking about The Man. Her memoir was invaluable to me as I went through the self-editing process, making sure I used the right insider terms and had the correct grasp on how the industry works. Honestly, I need to thank all the wrestlers who do interviews. I watched so many in preparation for writing this book. Let's just say I have an immense amount of respect for everything that goes into putting on a great match for the fans.

Okay, so this might be a little odd, but I need to acknowledge Bianca Belaire, Bayley, and their January 5, 2024, match on Smackdown. I watched that match over and over again to get ideas for the moves, taunts, and commentator dialogue. You two are also an inspiration, being dominating forces in the women's division. It's really cool to see such skill and talent on the roster.

I exhausted myself creating this book between all the research, planning, and actual writing. Through it all, I had my wife. From encouragement to working through plot holes to giving me this idea in the first place, I couldn't have done it without you.

Other Books from Ylva Publishing

www.ylva-publishing.com

Good Enough to Eat

Jae & Alison Grey

ISBN: 978-3-95533-242-6
Length: 223 pages (64,000 words)

Robin is a vampire who wants to change her eating habits. To fight her cravings for O negative, she goes to an AA meeting, where she meets Alana, who battles her own demons.

Despite their determination not to get involved, the attraction is undeniable.

Is it love or just bloodlust that makes Robin think Alana looks good enough to eat? Will it even matter once Alana finds out who Robin really is?

Ex-Wives of Dracula

Georgette Kaplan

ISBN: 978-3-95533-410-9
Length: 338 pages (122,000 words)

Mindy's best friend, Lucia, is a vampire. Every second Mindy spends with her she's in danger of becoming dinner. But Lucia needs help. To keep her alive they need fresh blood, and to cure her they have to kill her sire. So why is it that Nosferatu, the cops, and the chance of becoming an unwilling blood donor don't scare Mindy half as much as the way she feels when Lucia looks at her?

About Elaine J Daniels

Elaine J Daniels writes the stories she wants to read. For as long as she can remember, she has imagined vivid characters with extraordinary lives and adventures. Her first attempt at writing a novel was a retelling of Lord of the Rings with herself as the protagonist (and Frodo's girlfriend) when she was 11.

Currently residing in the American South, Elaine uses her communications background at a nonprofit. After her 9 to 5 job, she focuses on her writing career. Being a queer Southerner is a core part of Elaine's identity and she's passionate about advocating for progressive protections for the LGBTQ community.

When she's not writing, Elaine enjoys reading romance novels, eating her wife's cooking, trying new hobbies, and spending quality time with her friends, family, and furry babies.

CONNECT WITH ELAINE

Facebook: www.facebook.com/profile.php?id=61557143963401

E-Mail: authorelainedaniels@gmail.com

Pinned by Love

ISBN: 978-3-96324-975-4

Available in paperback and e-book formats.

Published by Ylva Publishing, legal entity of Ylva Verlag, e.Kfr.

Ylva Verlag, e.Kfr.
Owner: Astrid Ohletz
Am Kirschgarten 2
65830 Kriftel
Germany

www.ylva-publishing.com

First edition: 2025

Credits
Edited by Sarah Smeaton and Michelle Aguilar
Cover Design by Ronja Forleo
Print Layout by Streetlight Graphics

www.ingramcontent.com/pod-product-compliance
Lightning Source LLC
LaVergne TN
LVHW041027150826
845672LV00001B/239

* 9 7 8 3 9 6 3 2 4 9 7 5 4 *